Dreams in the Golden Country

The Diary of Zipporah Feldman, a Jewish Immigrant Girl

BY KATHRYN LASKY

Scholastic Inc. New York

Lower East Side, New York City
1903

I am sitting here on the wood suitcase, the one with the metal straps. Mama says I am too heavy to rest on the wicker one. It seems as if we have been in this baggage room forever, although it has only been two hours since we got off the boat. My oldest sister, Tovah, says to get used to it. It takes a long time to get "processed." I am not sure what this word means. I know when you enter life you are born, but when you enter America you are processed, here at Ellis Island. It has something to do with all the papers Mama carries with her. It also has a lot to do with waiting.

Tovah finds out a lot, for she roams all over this place. She is very nosy. She picks up gossip. She brings back scary stories about something called "inspection" that they will do to us in the next room. If we fail inspection we can be detained, made to wait, or even get sent back. And then when shall we ever see Papa again?

It has been nearly two years since we have seen him. He came to America before us to make enough money to buy our tickets on the ship. Every month he went to the draft-and-passage office and exchanged his American money for the ten rubles that he sent to us for our steerage voyage from Hamburg to New York. That is where the boat left from — Hamburg, Germany.

But first we had to travel there. For we are from Zarichka, a little village in Minsk Gubernia in Russia. I will tell you more about that later. My name is Zipporah Feldman, Zippy for short. I am Jewish. I am twelve. I am the youngest of three children. Miriam is fifteen and Tovah is seventeen. I weigh eighty-nine pounds on the kosher butcher scales (that is another story how Miriam and I sneaked into Reb Gulden's shop and weighed ourselves). Anyhow I am coming to America. No, not coming. I am finally here. And I am just now starting this diary. Mama gave me the diary before we left Zarichka. I am writing it in Yiddish, but I swear on the blessed memory of my grandmother that a year from now I shall be writing in English.

Same day, one hour later
Registry Room, Ellis Island

We are now in the biggest room I have ever been in. There are many long aisles. Mama is leaning against

Tovah with her head on her shoulder and snoring as we wait. Her *sheidel* has slipped down toward her eyebrow. She looks funny. Miriam and I giggle and wonder if we should fix it for her. Tovah says we should fix the wig by taking it off. She says in New York Jewish wives walk around in their own hair not wigs. She is sure of this. She says only in the old country is it considered vain to show your hair. This must be one of the ideas she picked up at the café in Zarichka where she and all her smarty friends went. Tovah thinks she knows everything. What she doesn't know she makes up. But I shouldn't make fun of her. All her snooping around here has helped us. She told us right before we walked up the stairs to this room that we should step lively and look energetic, because the medical inspectors watch you as you climb the stairs. If you are slow or lame, the doctors might disqualify you. Shut the door to America right in your face. We did well on the stairs. Now our line starts to move. The doctors will look at us. Let's hope we pass.

One hour later

If I ever criticize Tovah again may I be left speechless. May the Uppermost One make my tongue drop from my mouth. Here is what happened and how Tovah saved me. The doctors — they come up to you. The women go into a line where there is a nurse as well. They unbutton your collar to check for the neck swelling called goiter. They look in your ears and next check for bad backs or lameness. The worst part is the eye examination. They take a buttonhook and flip up your eyelid. There is a bad disease called trachoma and if you have it they send you back. Well, they flipped up my eyelid and then the nurse lady takes a piece of chalk and marks a letter on my back. E for eye in English. I have no eye disease at all. The day before we landed a piece of soot from the ship's smokestacks blew into my eye and caused a redness. When the nurse wrote this letter on my back my mother gave a little scream. I froze. Miriam looked as if she might faint, but Tovah quickly pushed me forward. I will never know how she did it, but faster than a shooting star she turned my coat with the chalk mark inside out. Before we knew it the man at the last medical table had stamped our papers. We quickly passed through the mental exam. There was an interpreter but Mama became quite huffy when they asked her if she was married. She began munching her lips and then she exploded in Yiddish, "What does this piece of disturbance take me for? I stand here with my three daughters and he asks if I am married." That is Mama's main curse, to call someone "a piece of disturbance." Or if she knows their nationality she calls them a Polish piece of disturbance or a Galician piece or an Italian piece.

Now all our papers are stamped. Tovah says we are safe. We do not have the letters LPN stamped on any one of them. LPN means liable to become a public nuisance. I look at us and wonder: Mama with her wig still not straight and her ankles swollen from standing so long in so many lines. Tovah, her direct honest eyes taking in everything. Miriam, like an angel with her almost blond hair curling around her lovely high forehead. And me, confused, skinnier than ever from throwing up all the way across the Atlantic. I think, how could we ever become a public nuisance? Are there four more unlikely people? Wait, I must stop writing. Our name is being called. Papa must be here!!

September 2, 1903
Lower East Side, New York City
14 Orchard Street

I feel totally, completely lost. I am not in Russia, but I don't know where I am. If this is America I don't like it, not one bit. Tovah forbids me to say that I hate it until I have lived here at least two years. She says it is unfair to make up one's mind that quickly.

Well, she might forbid me to say it but I can write it. It actually would take me forever to list all the things I hate, but first of all I think I hate change. And everything is changed. Even Papa. He no longer wears his sidelocks. Mama is shocked, I can tell. But he says when he lived in St. Petersburg as a young music student he never wore sidelocks. He says he can still be an Orthodox Jew without his *pe'ye*. But I know it disturbs Mama. She keeps muttering the words from Leviticus: "Thou shall not round the corners of your heads, neither shalt thou mar the corners of thy beard." This is the reason found in the Bible for why Jews do not cut their sidelocks. I don't care about the Bible reasons. I like Papa with *pe'ye*. They were soft and fuzzy and the color of the pale flames in a fire. His beard was always shorter than most Jewish men because of playing the violin. And Tovah was right. Many women do not wear wigs. They go about in their own hair, not even a scarf. That doesn't bother me. Besides Mama won't change. I know that for sure. Papa, however, *has* changed.

But worse than Papa's sidelocks is this place. It is awful, this tenement apartment. I cannot believe that back in Russia everyone called America the *Goldeneh Medina* — the Golden Country. There is nothing golden. It is only darkness. We entered a hall so skinny that fat Gittle from Petchenka Street could never have fit. Bad smells swirled around us. There are gaslights in the hall, but because the landlord tries to save money he will not turn them on until it is completely dark outside. But it is always completely dark inside. The staircase is narrow and rickety. When we got to our apartment, before we entered, Papa proudly pointed to a door in the hallway. It is the lavatory. We share it with the other family on our floor, the Sheehans. He says we are lucky to have such a luxury. Yes, so we enter this place, our apartment. Again, he tells us we are lucky. We have not just two rooms like most, we have three rooms: a parlor, a kitchen, and a dark, windowless bedroom. We three girls will sleep in the parlor and Mama and Papa in the back room.

Later

I just noticed this heap on a bed by the stove. It is a little old man with long sidelocks wrapped in circles around his ears. He wears a long black robe and a fur hat. Except for the fur he looks like a bag of bones, chicken bones, he is so small.

"And where does he sleep?" My mother's voice is wavy, as if it floats on a sea of tears. "Oh, this is Reb Simcha." Papa's voice is tense. "A religious scholar of great genius," my father whispered. My mother has always been in awe of *gaons*. She dreamed of having a son who would become a *gaon*. But instead there was this little bag of chicken bones sitting on a makeshift bed. "He's a boarder, isn't he, Yekl?"

"Yeah, yeah, but a *gaon*, too!" My mother looks thoughtful. I wonder if she really thinks we are so lucky? Yet all the time Mama keeps saying how lucky we are. And Tovah and Miriam, too. They look at me as if I am too young to know the meaning of lucky. We are lucky because the pogroms, when the Tsar's armies and, more often, the Russian peasants came through and killed people in the Jewish villages, never quite reached Zarichka. And we are lucky because Papa left for America before he could be drafted into the Tsar's army. And we are lucky because we saw what happened during the last Passover season we all celebrated together in Zarichka, the one when the people from Zlinka staggered into our village with their terrible wounds. A group of peasants and soldiers filled up with vodka had set out to kill them with scythes and axes and clubs. There was a girl Miriam's age. Her head was all bandaged. Her mother told us that her ear had been cut off by a scythe! That was the Passover when Papa said we would leave. First he went and now we follow. So it all began on Passover of the year 1901. I was just ten years old. I had two ears then. I still have them. So, yes, I guess I am lucky.

But am I lucky to live with a smelly little bag of chicken bones who incidentally is a genius? Lucky to live in a three-room apartment with one window? Lucky to have running water in the hall when we had a whole brook running just outside our house in Zarichka? Lucky to live in a place that is so dark that when I go to bed at night and wake in the morning I do not believe that there is such a thing called a sky?

Yes, I am one lucky girl, am I not?

What a day! It is Thursday and Mama finally, after much pleading, allowed us to go out shopping, or else how would we have food to fix for our first *Shabbos* dinner in America? So Papa drew a map for us to the Pig Market on Hester Street. I can't believe they call it the Pig Market and the place is swollen with Jews. Miriam says maybe it's a joke because it is said that you can buy everything except a pig there — suspenders, pants, hats, spectacles, peaches, chickens, geese, fresh bread, stale bread. And there are soda vendors. We bought a carp, a big fresh-looking fellow. We know how to look a fish in the eye and tell how long it's been dead. And no one ever better try and sell Tovah one with a cloudy eye, as the first pushcart man did. He swore up and down that the carp had just come out of the water. He swore in Yiddish first, then Polish, and then finally he swore in Russian. Not one language could convince Tovah, but imagine his surprise when Tovah speaks back to him in perfect English (at least it sounded that way to me), "What do you take me for, a greenhorn?" As I should have suspected, Tovah has been studying English secretly for the last several months. We finally bought a carp from the lady with a pushcart next to the lady who churned horseradish.

It was Miriam's idea to get the horseradish. "What will we put it on?" I say. "It is too strong for carp." "Not for fish," Miriam says, "for Reb Simcha. We put it on him." We all laughed. You see, he smells so bad we think the horseradish might cut the sickly ripeness of him. I wish he would spend one tenth of the time he does in the prayer house at the public baths. We are going tomorrow morning first thing to get nice and pinky clean for *Shabbos*.

September 4, 1903

Less than an hour until sunset, so not much time to write. Even Tovah agreed not to try to sneak any time as she usually does with her studies and thus break the *Shabbos* by writing. If it weren't for the food and the singing, *Shabbos* could be very boring. You cannot write or sew or cut or kindle a fire or even tie knots. It is forbidden. Papa says there is a nice non-Jew, a *Shabbos goy*, who will come and turn the gaslights low for us. He is a relative of the Sheehans. The Sheehans' children are too young to do it, mostly babies. There is a lot of yelling and squalling. We can hear it through the air shaft. The air shaft is for ventilation for the lavatory and the back bedroom spaces. It runs up and down through the middle of the building. We should put Reb Simcha in the air shaft. I do not understand any of the words yet that the Sheehans scream at one another. The grandmother screams a lot.

Tovah has promised to help me learn English, but I shall be going to a school, I think. Miriam and Tovah will be going to work, probably in one of the sweatshops. Tovah would prefer a real factory. Mama and Papa say I am absolutely too young to work. There is a school on Mott Street. We passed near it today when we went for our baths. After our baths we picked up the *challah* from the baker and then we came to back to our horrid little apartment. It started to seem just the tiniest bit like our little stone cottage in Zarichka, for the same *Shabbos* smells started to float through the air. Right now I can smell the *lekache* baking. The sweet lemony smell sweeps through the parlor where I write and I just hope that Reb Simcha does not come home too soon and spoil it all.

"Twenty minutes to *licht bentschen*," Miriam just called out. Then Mama will say the blessing and light the *Shabbos* candles, just before sunset. I hope Papa gets home soon. The *Shabbos* table even in this grim apartment looks lovely with the white tablecloth, the two loaves of *challah*, and the candles. The apartment grows darker and darker but Tovah really put a shine on the candlesticks and the *kiddush* cup. They gleam so brightly and on this our first Sabbath in America I can almost believe that there is a sky.

September 8, 1903

It has been so many days since I have written. What with *Shabbos* I stopped, of course, but once *Shabbos* was over — I don't know, I just couldn't get back to writing. I am having many confusing thoughts. When I read my last entry I realize that I had high hopes for *Shabbos*. But again, it was different here than back in Zarichka. You see, Papa didn't go to the synagogue, and there is a *shul* quite near. I think Mama was upset, but in some ways it was nicer. We ate earlier and we had more time to sing. We sang all four stanzas of "Shalom Aleichem," Peace Unto You, each stanza at least two times. We danced around the table as we always do. The only bad part was that Reb Simcha came back during the last stanza and that little bag of bones squeezed into the circle and took my hand and Papa's. His skin feels like chicken, too, plucked chicken, moist and puckery. He even dances like one, little jerky hopping steps. You'd think he only had three toes on each foot.

And then Papa, before *kiddush,* the wine blessing, was recited, sang the beautiful words of "Ayshet Chayil." This is the song to the wife, the song to the homemaker, the woman of valor, and usually Mama beams as he sings the verses. But this time she just sort of sat there and looked, well, rather dull, beaten down. Then he sang the *kiddush.* I think this country might be too much for Mama, but what have we got to go back to? There is news of another horrible pogrom in the state of Minsk. Eight hundred people killed. I know Mama is upset about the new ways here, about Papa not going to *shul* and him shaving his sidelocks and all the women who go out in their own hair. But at least that hair is attached to a head and that head is attached to a body. It does seem silly to get upset about wigs and such when it could be so much worse. As Tanta Fruma of the thousand proverbs used to say, "Better a Jew without a beard than a beard without a Jew."

So, it is not comfortable, this situation with Mama and Papa. Papa works so hard. I sneaked a look at his violin — covered in a thick layer of dust. I don't think he has played it since he arrived here two years ago. He has worked as much as eighteen hours a day to make money in the sweatshop, sewing cloaks to bring us over, and now we are here and Mama and Papa stare at each other like strangers. I am tired now and sad. I should not be so sad, I guess, for as Tanta Fruma always said, "Better a bad peace than a good war." It is just a bad peace between Mama and Papa right now. Maybe things will improve.

I forgot that one of the best parts of *Shabbos* was the *Shabbos goy*. He is so nice and very handsome. His name is Sean O'Malley. He is very funny and knows everything that is going on in this entire city. He is a fireman, but Friday is his night off. His father is also a fireman and his grandfather was a policeman. He explained to Tovah what the Sheehans fight about. Mrs. Sheehan is from Belfast in Northern Ireland and Mr. Sheehan and his mother are from Limerick. And the north and the south parts of Ireland hate each other and the grandmother suspects Mrs. Sheehan of being a Protestant. But she is not. She is a Catholic.

Well, I am to start school next Monday. Miriam started yesterday to work in the same shop as Papa, and Tovah found work in a shirtwaist factory. She pulls basting threads. One day in the factory and she is an expert. She comes home with tales of how the owner is a disgusting man who is exploiting the workers, and it needs to be a union shop. I do not know what this means.

Tovah is really flying with the English. She brings home newspapers to read and she is teaching me. I like reading the newspapers. The headline words are nice and big and there are pictures. I have learned the word "typhoid." It is a disease and there is a lady called Typhoid Mary. She has been spreading this disease. She works in jobs involved with handling food. That is why she is so dangerous. But Tovah says that we need not worry since we eat only kosher food and Typhoid Mary is not Jewish, so she would never be working in a place where we buy our food. I like learning English this way. So here are the new words I learned: *Typhoid, Infection, Health, Department of Health, Spread*. Tovah is making me up a verb chart and then I am going to be writing sentences using verbs, probably mostly about disease.

Only fifteen minutes till *licht bentschen,* then three more hours until *licht Seanschen*: That's when Sean O'Malley comes to turn low the gas flames and damper the wood-stove. I told Miriam my made-up phrase . . . *licht Seanschen*. She blushed. Thank goodness we're not having carp this week. We're having chicken stew. In any case, I won't have to sing the fishy song. You see, when I was little, every time Mama served fish I used to sing this song about fishies swimming in the Ptich, that was the river near our village. Anyhow, it's a very dumb song. Maybe it's cute when you're seven or eight, but dumb when you're twelve. Still, Papa wanted me to sing it since he had been away from us so long. So I did. Reb Simcha smiled at me and drooled and I saw that he only has about four teeth in his mouth. Six minutes until *licht bentschen,* and Mama says that the *kiddush* cup is not filled with wine yet. She likes everything set before she lights the candles and says the blessing. Or as she puts it she likes everything to be *shabbosdik,* in the spirit of *Shabbos.*

Bye-bye for the next twenty-four hours or so.

September 14, 1903

I have never felt more completely lost. And humiliated, far beyond blushing. Why? Because they put me in a class with mostly six- and seven-year-olds at school. It is the first-grade classroom. I barely fit in the chair. This is what they do for immigrant children who don't speak English. I am miserable — totally, completely miserable. This is such misery, such *tsores*. I am *tsoredik*. I am going to make a list of every Yiddish word I know for misery, pain, and sadness:

> *tsores*
> *umetik*
> *veytik*
> *di yesurim*

There — I feel better.

September 15, 1903

School is still horrible. A snotty little seven-year-old made fun of my accent when we said the Pledge of Allegiance to the flag. I am miserable. I shall find some more words to put on my misery list. I might branch out to include words for disgusting. For that little seven-year-old was a *paskudnyak* lump of a thing. What a piece of disturbance!

Later that night

Tovah found out about my misery list. She says I am a fool. I should not be making lists of Yiddish words for misery. That I should be making the list in English. And then she quotes Tanta Fruma for five minutes on fools and I am so mad I argue back each time:

Tovah: A fool remains a fool.

Me: There's an exception to every rule.

Tovah: Better to be a wise person in hell than a fool in paradise.

Me: This is paradise, Tovah? This rotten little apartment with smelly Reb Chicken Bones!

Then Tovah got mad and turned red. I didn't know what she might do, but she went to the cupboard and poured something into a spoon. She came back and in the nastiest, meanest voice she said, "Taste this." And I was so scared I opened my mouth. It was honey. I was surprised completely. "Don't look like such a block-head. You are a *goylem*," she said. I swallowed the sweetness, for this was what they did on a boy's first day of religious school. In *cheder* for each Hebrew letter whose name the boy would say correctly a drop of honey was placed on his tongue, so learning would always be sweet. But never for girls. Tovah must have read my thoughts. "In America learning in schools is not just for boys." I saw Miriam watching us and her eyes filled with tears. I knew then that she would rather be crunched into a small chair with a classroom of six-year-olds than working in the shop with Papa. I felt bad in spite of the honey in my mouth.

September 16, 1903

Oh, glory. I brim with *glik*. I know the word now in English: happiness. Guess what? A girl just my age came into my class. She is even taller than I am. Her name is Bluma. Bluma Wolf. But she says call her Blu for short. She is German Jewish, so she doesn't speak Yiddish, or hardly any at all. None of the German Jews do. But they can understand a lot because Yiddish is so close to German. She lived in a town close to the Polish border, so she speaks a kind of Germanized Polish or Polishized German. So we get along because, of course, Zarichka was close to the Polish border. And guess what else? She lives, you won't believe this, three doors down — number 20 Orchard Street! We're neighbors.

September 17, 1903

Blu and I walked home from school today through the Pig Market. I had to pick up some turnips and some fresh-ground horseradish for Mama for *Shabbos*. Now that Tovah and Miriam are working all day long I get sent on a lot of errands. Mama is still scared to go out by herself. We had some extra pennies so we bought some pickles to eat and some soda water. We sat on the corner of Hester and Ludlow and ate our pickles and sipped our soda right out in front of the soda shop. We can understand each other pretty well. I told her about Typhoid Mary and not to worry about the soda or the pickles, because it was all kosher. I did a very good imitation of how Reb Simcha eats. Blu says I should be an actress. It's easy to imitate him. He sort of munches his lips along with the food. Amazing he has any lips left.

We went to her apartment. She has two little brothers and one sister. She is the oldest. There is a baby just six months old, then a four-year-old, an eight-year-old, and then Blu who is a month older than I am. Her father has a pushcart. He sells suspenders mostly. He was a photographer back in Germany and took pictures of very fancy people. Weddings and dignitaries. It is sad for men to have to come here and do something so different. Like Papa. His first love was the violin and music. Now here is Papa, no music, dust on the violin, working in a sweatshop. At least Uncle Moishe, Mama's brother, works at Brooks Brothers. But he's a better tailor than Papa. Papa had to learn how to sew when he got here. Uncle Moishe already knew how and has been here much longer. Uncle Moishe is already a citizen. I can't believe I have an uncle who is a citizen of the United States of America. Anyhow, enough of that. I have found a friend and Blu and I swear that we shall study English so hard that by *Hanukkah* we shall be promoted to at least the third grade and by *Purim* fourth grade and by the end of the year seventh grade, where we belong with other twelve-year-olds. Now, I won't be able to write for a while because tomorrow is *Shabbos* and then we go right into the High Holy Days, *Rosh Hashanah* and *Yom Kippur*. But I can't wait because right after that is *Sukkot* and Papa says we shall build a *sukkah* booth on the fire escape!!

September 23, 1903

Barely time to write. We are cooking constantly and then there is the time I spend in *shul*. We went to Reb Simcha's synagogue over on Norfolk Street. *Rosh Hashanah* celebrates the beginning of the New Year and fresh starts. When the time came to return the Torah to the ark, when the ram's horn is blown, guess who blew it? Reb Simcha! He turned bright red as he blew the *shofar*. His cheeks puffed out like immense tomatoes, and tears streamed from his eyes. Tovah and Miriam and I crowded toward the screen that separates the women's section from the men's, so we could see better. Now I feel guilty about all my nasty thoughts about him. What if Reb Simcha has a heart attack and dies blowing the *shofar* for the New Year? *Oy*! And there is still another service where he must blow the *shofar*! I never knew *Rosh Hashanah* could be so tense.

September 24, 1903

Reb Simcha lives. He got through all the services — well over a hundred blasts on the *shofar*. But then Miriam and I could barely keep from giggling when we saw him turning bright pink in the last service. We simply could not look at each other or we would die laughing. Now *Yom Kippur* comes. Then *Sukkot*! Hooray! Papa keeps warning us not to think about our lovely *sukkah* booths back in Russia with alder and birch branches. I have yet to see a leaf in this city, let alone a whole tree. But Blu says there are trees in parks. Someday we plan to go to one.

October 2, 1903

Good news! Teacher says that Blu and I are making very good progress and that there is a chance we shall be promoted to third grade even before *Hanukkah*. We study every afternoon after school and sometimes in the evenings. I prefer studying at our house in the evenings as I find Blu's father somewhat strange, well, not strange just cold. He always has his nose buried in a newspaper, and if the baby cries he says to his wife, "Make it stop." *"It,"* he calls his own child. *"It."* Is that not strange? "It" is a little boy named Emmanuel.

P.S. I should be able to study harder now that the High Holy Days are over. More time, more food. After fasting on *Yom Kippur*, all the next day I felt as if my brains had floated out of my head. I guess that is what they mean when they say one feels light-headed.

October 3, 1903

When I was in the lavatory this morning I heard the Sheehans yelling as usual and I finally understood one English word. No, two. "Little Protestant." It was the old grandma and she really spat the words out. When I came out of the lavatory Mrs. Sheehan was running down the hall crying, and the grandma was glaring at her. The grandmother looks awful. She has no teeth, so her face collapses around her mouth. There is no mouth, really, just a dark hole that is sucked in and spits out words. Mr. Sheehan just stood in the doorway looking one second at his wife and the next at his mother as if he didn't know which side to choose. Then he started coughing and went inside. He's very sickly looking. I would hate to be married to someone like that — sick, can't make up his mind. But he should be on his wife's side.

October 4, 1903

Am I not good writing this first time in English? Here is what I want to say. There is a boy who is a true pain. His name is Yitchak Silver.

I have to switch back to Yiddish now because I am not fluent enough to tell you how really annoying this boy is. He got here a year ago and he is already in eighth grade. He thinks he knows everything. A real *macher.* Mr. Big Wheel! And he's at least an inch shorter than either Blu or me. Now here's the problem. He's invited himself over to help us build our *sukkah* booth tomorrow on the fire escape. Says he can get some good bamboo poles and branches. Here's how he talks: "I got this connection with a copper (his slang for policeman) on Delancey Street. He can fix me up with some good materials through a brother-in-law." Just at that minute Tovah walks up. She says to him, "Oh sure, of course, you must come." They start blabbing away in English in front of Blu and me. I felt it was very rude. Then he turns to me and says something in English that I don't understand but later Tovah translated. He said your sister is a "smart cookie," meaning Tovah because of her good English. "Smart cookie!" What a stupid expression. Something tells me that English is going to be somewhat of a disappointment after Yiddish.

In spite of Yitzy (that's his nickname) we did have fun putting together the *sukkah* on the fire escape. More helpful than Yitzy was Sean O'Malley! Yitzy did bring some wood poles, but Sean apparently had gone up-town and snitched some branches for us with beautiful turning leaves — orange and red and gold.

Tovah has joined an organization called the Yiddishe Yugend. They supposedly discuss the problems of the world and the terrible conditions of the sweat-shops. Mama says she thinks all they do is go to the Café Royale on Second Avenue and 12th Street and spend their money on coffee and pastry. Tovah better watch it that Typhoid Mary doesn't get a job in their kitchen. Tovah only makes $5.20 a week and she brings all of it home. So I don't think she's eating out much. Anyhow, she brought home one of her friends from the group, Mandy Levin. He looks like a wild man. Hair sticking straight out all over his head. If it were red he would look like a fire burning out of control. He was nice, though. He and Yitzy with Sean's help got the *sukkah* up in no time. Then the fun part came. Putting on the branches. Blu's younger sister made paper chains. Blu, Miriam, and I made paper leaves. Papa was right. It wasn't the same kind of *sukkah*. Not as beautiful perhaps and no fragrant evergreens. But there was one interesting thing: In Russia I took the stars for granted. Here I don't. Yitzy, Sean, and Mandy stayed for dinner in the *sukkah*. Food tastes better outside. Then it started to rain, so we went in.

October 7, 1903

Heard grouchy old Mrs. Sheehan yelling again across the air shaft. Caught more words, but had to ask Tovah to translate. She yelled at her daughter-in-law something about a "sneaky little Protestant smile." I didn't know what sneaky was. Tovah explained. I feel so sorry for the young Mrs. Sheehan to have to live with that piece of disturbance. And Mrs. Sheehan is Catholic just like the old lady, and Irish, so I don't understand. Just because she's from a different part of Ireland, it shouldn't make a difference.

The other English I learned was from a sign on a store over on Broadway when I walked with Tovah. It said IRISH NEED NOT APPLY. It seems sad to see such a sign in this country, which is supposed to be a democracy. Tovah says unions will change all that.

October 8, 1903

These days are fun. For almost every night during *Sukkot* we have had a guest. Just when I thought Yitzy was getting tolerable he goes and does such a Yitzy-ish thing. Tovah is talking about what she likes most about *Sukkot*, that it is so democratic — all Jews, rich or poor, are asked to eat in a simple shelter, just like the Jews who wandered in the desert with Moses for forty years. I said that as far as I could tell there weren't any rich Jews around here. Well, Yitzy breaks in. "Ah, uptown!" he says. "There are a lot of rich Jews uptown, German Jews." Tovah thinks these Jews are bad. She says they are responsible for what is called the sweating system that allows the sweatshops and all the terrible conditions in the factories. How's this? I asked. She says it's because the Germans think they are too good to hold a needle or a scissors and they get other people to do it. They are contractors and don't care about the conditions of the workers. They want to distance themselves from not just manual labor but from all Jewish immigrants. But they were immigrants, I say. "They came here earlier. Much earlier," says Yitzy. "They know more about being American." Tovah just snorts. "We embarrass them," says Tovah. "They don't have any accents," says Yitzy. "Not a trace. They speak English like real Yankees." Then he starts going on about the Freed family and the Warburg family and the Baumgolds. And how he's got a connection with this one and that one. He is a thirteen-year-old boy, just had his *bar mitzvah* six months ago. Now you tell me how this *bar mitzvah* boy knows all these uptown folks?

October 9, 1903

Uncle Moishe came for dinner in the *sukkah* last night. It is only the second time we have seen him since we've been here, except at *Yom Kippur* services but that doesn't count because we only saw him from the women's section and then he rushed right off. He got a promotion at Brooks Brothers. He and Yitzy hit it off famously. Yitzy says he wishes his father would get a job at Brooks Brothers. His father is a designer in a small factory and according to Yitzy the factory owes its success to his father's talent in copying "uptown" fashions in cloaks for men. But the owners of the factory treat everyone miserably. They play favorites and never trust anyone, and often do not let them go to the toilet. And they threaten to fire them all the time if they are just one minute late to work. If Mama is upset about Papa and no sidelocks she should take a good, hard look at Uncle Moishe. Not only no sidelocks, he is not wearing his ritual fringes.

Later the same evening

Mama noticed. She wailed, "My own dear brother has lost his soul threads." That's what Mama calls the *tzitzit*, for they are supposed to remind men to observe all the commandments and all the Jewish laws for leading a blessed life. Papa didn't say anything. He just went over and gave her a pat on the shoulder. But there was something in his eyes that made me wince a little. I think perhaps Papa has been thinking of taking off his fringes. "Next thing you know," Mama said, "he won't be wearing his skullcap." Well, he doesn't. I saw him take the *yarmulke* off as soon as he left that night, when he was halfway down the first flight of stairs.

October 10, 1903

Guess what Miriam and Tovah and I did last night? Slept outside. The weather suddenly turned hot for October. Sean told Miriam that folks sleep out on the roof all the time in the hot weather. So we climbed right up there. If you lie flat on your back you can see nothing but sky and stars.

October 15, 1903

I am sick with worry. Just when I thought things were getting a little better between Mama and Papa they get worse. Just when I thought this was the most wonderful *Sukkot,* with every evening Mandy or Sean or Blu coming over, even Yitzy — I mean, he is entertaining — everything falls apart. Mama is furious because Papa didn't go to *shul* for *Simchat Torah* services that mark the end of *Sukkot.* It was such a nice service, too. Here in this *shul* in America when they bring the Torah around they let the women reach through the screen or over it and touch the Torah. It was very exciting. Women never touch the Torah in the old country.

We thought we were supposed to meet Papa at the

synagogue. When we get home, he comes in a moment later full of apologies. He forgot! His boss got many bundles. The bundles are the pieces to be made into cloaks. Workers in the shop compete to get bundles and he gave Papa three. And Papa just got so carried away he forgot. "So you forgot the blessed Torah for the blessed cloaks!" Mama spat out the words. He put down the money he had made, for it was payday. It was a large stack of dollar bills — almost twenty-five. This is the most money Papa has ever made in a week. But Mama just stared at it as if it were dirt, animal droppings, *dreck*!

October 19, 1903

The argument goes on and on between Mama and Papa. Every night for three days. I can practically say their lines.

Mama: I thought I married a pious man.

Papa: No, Sarah, you married a musician whom you thought would turn into a pious man.

Mama: May I be left blind if I did not think when I looked at you playing your violin the first time in Zarichka that this was a pious man. May I have one hundred years of blackness upon me!

Papa: Don't curse yourself, Sarah. This is America, Sarah.

Mama: I curse Columbus.

Papa: He's dead already.

Mama: And a good thing. Not soon enough, not before 1492.

This startles me. How does Mama know the year Columbus discovered America? Oh, well, I am too sad to think.

October 20, 1903

Last night after Mama and Papa's fight when we three girls climbed into bed Tovah was asleep in a minute, but Miriam and I lay awake. Miriam could tell how upset I was and put her arms around me and tried to comfort me. It worked for a moment, but then just as I was on that funny, milky little border between waking and sleeping I had a sudden and terrible thought. I jerked awake. "What is it? Zipporah?" Miriam whispered. "Oh, Miriam, what if Mama and Papa get divorced and Mama marries Reb Simcha because he is such a pious man?"

"Don't be ridiculous, Zippy. They are not going to get divorced and there is no way that Mama is going to marry Reb Simcha. She complains about him smelling just as much as we do."

Then I say, "She'd clean him up."

Nothing Miriam can tell me helps. Finally, she says that it is warm in the apartment and let's take some blankets and our shawls to the roof. So we do. It is chilly but I have a good night's sleep.

October 21, 1903

Sleeping on the roof is good for me. I feel better. I think better. I am figuring things out between Mama and Papa. First of all I have figured out that Mama is truly mixed up. Much more so than me. They need to compromise. Miriam agrees and so does Tovah. I ask them both, do they think it is very odd that Mama knew about Columbus the other night? Mama has no real book learning. She can read but she only reads the prayer book, and the labels on bottles or the signs for sales. So I conclude she must have peeked into one of my schoolbooks. "So?" Tovah says as only Tovah can say "so," as if to puncture any thought you might have so it deflates like a tired old balloon. But I say, "So! Does this not give you the idea that perhaps Mama is curious?"

"About what?" Miriam asks.

"Columbus?" says Tovah.

"Not only that but about what I am learning in school and maybe she feels left out. Look, she is here all day, alone. I go to school. You two and Papa go to work. Reb Simcha goes to *shul* and does whatever they pay him there to do — clean up, sweep, whatever. She stays here, thinking about Zarichka and how life will never be the same again."

"But she is scared to go out by herself," Tovah says.

I know that is true, I explain, but I think perhaps we must bring some life to her and then she will stop worrying about Papa and his piety. So this was my compromise: We should rent a sewing machine for Mama. She sews beautifully. She should begin custom dressmaking. Papa, in turn, will agree to go to *shul* more often and never skip his morning prayers, as he has done. And I will help Mama with the dressmaking, find clients for her, and maybe I shall begin to share some of my schoolbooks with her. Teach her some English. Miriam smiles and says what a wonderful idea. But Tovah just looks puzzled.

October 22, 1903

It rained last night so we could not sleep on the roof. But when I awoke in the middle of the night Miriam was gone. At first I thought she had just gone to the lavatory in the hall, but when she returned her hair was damp as if she had been outside.

October 23, 1903

Hope at last for Mama and Papa. I talked to Papa about the compromise and he thinks it is a very good idea. Then he went right out and with all the money he made on doing those extra bundles on *Simchat Torah* he rented a sewing machine. He got one for one dollar fifty cents per month. It is nearly a tenth of his usual weekly pay but I think it will be worth it. Mama hesitated at first. But then I told her that I could go out and do all the business for her and take orders here on the Lower East Side. Maybe Yitzy with his uptown connections could get her uptown work and she could start making some dresses. Papa said, "You will make us rich, Sarah. You are much better with a needle than I am."

"From your mouth to God's ears!" That was what

Tanta Fruma always said, and when Mama said that I knew that things were changing. So I jumped in. "Mama, it will be fun, you and me working together and I can teach you the English words for things like buttons, and thread, and hems, and bias cut, and sleeves, and collars." And then all of us reminded her of how beautifully she sews! And Mama lifted her apron and bursts into tears. Mama cried like a baby. You think she is going to die because she holds her breath. But she didn't die. She sat down at the sewing machine and touched it gently with her small hands. "So, what do you call this, Zipporah?" pointing to *de rod*.

"'Wheel,' Mama."

"And this?"

"'Treadle,' Mama."

"And this?"

"'Bobbin,' Mama."

And then, I really think of this as a miracle: Our little conversation seemed to fall into the cadences of a song, and I was so wrapped up in teaching Mama the English names that I did not see Papa go and fetch his violin, but suddenly this dark little room began to fill with the notes. They stole in softly, slowly winding through the dark shadows and small pools of light cast by the two gas fixtures. The music was so delicate it made me think of the slightest breeze that often stirred the grass at the edge of the Ptich River on a summer day. But no, not like the wind, really at all. More like butterflies. That is how these notes were — like beautiful, delicate butterflies that had escaped from a long-ago sunny day into the night of our tenement apartment on Orchard Street. The room began to shimmer with the music my father was making.

October 27, 1903

I had to wait a long time for young Mrs. Sheehan to come out of the lavatory this morning. While she was in there I heard these funny little sounds. When she came out I realized she had been crying. I feel so sorry for her. Sean told us that her husband lost his job, and Miriam said that she thinks Sean gives them the money he makes for being our *Shabbos goy* and turning down the gaslights.

November 1, 1903

What with school and getting Mama started sewing I have barely had time to write. But started she is and I must thank Yitzy for his help. Despite his help he is still very annoying. He says Blu and I are not making as much progress as he did. By this time last year he was in third grade! Through one of his "connections," however, he got an order for Mama. It's not exactly an uptown lady, but close. It's an uptown lady's children's governess. Yitzy knows someone who knows her through City College up on Lexington Avenue and 23rd Street. He says if she likes the work she'll tell her employer or maybe her friends at City College. It's a skirt and vest, but Yitzy says who knows? It could turn into a whole what he calls "ensemble," which I guess means a coat, too. I've never heard of women wearing coats that much. Mostly shawls. But Yitzy knows everything.

November 2, 1903

I am writing this in English. My English is getting a lot better because I really think helping Mama with the sewing is helping me with my English. I make a big effort to say not just one word but a whole sentence with a subject and a verb. So I say, "This is the thread for the bobbin."

November 3, 1903

Blu and I both want to be Marie Curie. She is going to receive the most important prize in the world for science. She is going to receive the Nobel Prize in physics for her work with her husband on uranium and radioactivity. I do not know how to explain these in Yiddish, forget English. I read about Marie in the newspaper that Tovah brings home and helps me translate.

November 8, 1903

Don't think I am giving up on writing in English. I am not at all. For at the moment I am writing a composition for school on Marie Curie. Finally something Yitzy is not an expert on — radioactivity and uranium! But Tovah's friend Mandy is. And guess what? This is so exciting. He took me and Tovah uptown to the library at City College. It is red brick and has ivy-covered walls and spires and I do believe you get smart just by putting one foot inside that college. For I did. Suddenly I began to understand the English that was being spoken around me, not all of it, not a lot of it, but a bit of a bit of it.

We saw many fashionable women uptown. The young ones who are the students at City College look very nice, too.

We have finished the skirt and vest for the governess so I hope she tells her college girlfriends.

November 13, 1903

Only thirty minutes until *licht bentschen* and things are happening just too fast so I don't know how I will have time to write. First, guess what? Blu and I have been promoted!! We start third grade on Monday! We are ahead of schedule by a whole month. *Hanukkah* doesn't start this year until December 14. I think the teacher was very impressed with my composition about Marie Curie. Also, the uptown governess has come back, not for her college girlfriends but for the entire household staff. The lady of the house wants new uniforms for the servants. The governess lady — oh, she has the most wonderful name, Caroline — says if we do a good job the lady might have us make some clothes for the children.

November 15, 1903

I spent all Sunday morning cutting. First collars for the uniforms for Mama's uptown job and then pictures of Marie Curie. Mandy brought over some other newspapers. I stick them to the wall above my bed with spirit gum or tailor's tape.

The Sheehans' youngest baby is very sick. We hear him wailing across the air shaft.

November 16, 1903

It feels so good to be in third grade. Blu and I are only a foot or so taller than the other kids. But Blu is not so happy. She says her parents are fighting all the time. I tried to suggest the compromise we did with my parents, which seems to be helping. But Blu says that is not the problem. Her mother doesn't care whether her father is pious or not. She just wants him to make more money, because now they are having another baby and she wants a bigger apartment. I think it would be hard to compromise with Mr. Wolf. He always has a sour look on his face and he never says anything.

November 17, 1903

Why can't everybody be happy at the same time and then sad at the same time? It would be easier. I am now happy and out of step, I think, for in addition to Blu being so upset, Yitzy is. He says his father is a *schnook*. I didn't know what he meant. So, what's a *schnook*? I ask. He says it's a *patsy*. So, what's a *patsy*? I ask. "You know," he says, "someone who gets taken advantage of." The boss in his father's factory charged him for some cloth that he claims he was shorted on in an order. Yitzy says the boss thinks his father is stealing material to make samples of his own. Yitzy wants him to quit and go to work for Brooks Brothers. But his father is very timid. Nothing like Yitzy.

November 19, 1903

I cannot stop thinking about Marie Curie. Imagine a woman being a scientist! We think it's so great because at the synagogue at *Simchat Torah* we were allowed to touch the Torah.

November 20, 1903

The Sheehans' baby died last night. It was so sad. Mrs. Sheehan is very poorly. We hear her crying all day, all night. Mama went over with some food and she helped clean up the other children. The old grandma is useless. The Irish ways of death are not like the Jewish ways. They do not bury the dead person immediately. They have a wake and they dress up the dead person very fancy and keep the person in the casket in the living room for people to see and say good-bye. Mama says we must all pay a call. I am dreading it. I do not want to look at a little dead baby boy.

November 21, 1903

Well, we all went and looked at the little Sheehan boy. It was not as bad as I thought. He looked beautiful as if he were sleeping. All clean with his hair neatly combed. He wore a little gray suit with a flower sticking out from under his collar. What was worse looking was that grandmother. She was muttering in some weird language. Sean later told us that she speaks Gaelic, or Irish sometimes. Mr. Sheehan just sat there — again looking back and forth between his wife and his mother as if trying to figure out which one to comfort. Poor Mrs. Sheehan. I just feel so sorry for her.

November 23, 1903

It feels easy now writing to you in English because guess what? When Shabbos *finishes I begin to write a letter to Marie Curie in English. You notice I only write in present tense. It is easier for me. I feel obliged to say* mazeltov, *congratulations, to Doctor Curie. She teaches at the Sorbonne in Paris. Mandy maybe knows the address. I hope she speaks English, because although I understand Polish, and she is born in Poland, I cannot write it. I do not think she speaks Yiddish. I tell her that she is a wonderful woman. That she is a wonderful scientist. That when I grow up I want to be a scientist. I ask her what course of study I should follow at City College. I ask her if she has ever heard of City College on 23rd Street and Lexington Avenue. I do not tell her that I am in the third grade. Now I am going to work even harder.*

November 24, 1903

I should bite my tongue. Mama and I were working today on the order for the uniforms for the uptown lady's servants. Mama is not wearing her wig but has a scarf covering her head and some of her hair sneaks out and I am thinking how young she looks, how much better she would look in her own hair. So I say, "Mama, why don't you think of going in your own hair? Blu's mama does." And she gives me a very dark look. Like this is no business of yours. So I quickly shut up. And then under her breath I hear her quote Tanta Fruma: "The greatest folly of a fool is when he thinks he's smart." Then, a few seconds later, another installment thanks to Tanta Fruma: "A mother's slap won't give a child a hole in the head." But even though she does not slap me, two Tanta Frumas in a row is like being spanked. I'll never speak again of the wig.

November 25, 1903

You will never guess what happened. Blu's father has disappeared. Left, gone, vanished! At first I said to Blu, you must go to the police, for I was thinking something terrible might have happened to him. You hear of thugs hitting people on the head for their money and leaving them for dead. Blu said that she told her mother the same thing, but her mother said, no, she knew that nothing like that had happened to him. He was simply gone. I asked, How does she know? Did he leave a note? Blu just shrugged her shoulders. I feel I cannot ask anymore. And her mother is expecting another baby and this is so awful. How will they live? And to think just yesterday I was telling Mama how Blu's mother didn't wear a wig. Now Mama will say, "See!"

November 26, 1903

I am so mad at Yitzy I could wring his neck. Blu and I were in the Pig Market doing errands. We were at our usual soda shop drinking soda and sharing a pickle, when Yitzy comes up. He sees that Blu's face is all blotchy from crying. Now wouldn't you think he'd take a hint and go away when I say that Blu has a private problem? No, not Yitzy. What's wrong with Blu? he asks. So we have to tell him and then Yitzy goes into a whole *megillah* all about his connections at the police department and how he knows somebody who knows somebody in the department of missing persons, and how he can mention it to a Mr. So and So. Well, Blu is so innocent and trusting, this actually raises her hopes. And what can I say? I know Yitzy, he's "talking through his hat" — that's an English expression I just learned and I love it. It means you know nothing about nothing. You just talk for the joy of hearing your own voice. That's Yitzy! I decided to change the subject real fast. "How's your father?" I ask. Complete silence. Not for long, though. He raises a finger, like some Talmudic scholar. "I want to talk to you about that," he says. And then adds, "But now is not the occasion." He just about tips his *yarmulke* to us, the way uptown fellas tip their hats, I am told, to ladies. I give Yitzy another six months with his *yarmulke*, and maybe four with the fringes.

November 27, 1903

Mama did not say "See!" when I told her about Mr. Wolf. Not even a word about the wig. She was very upset, though. She says Papa and Reb Simcha must take the case to the Beth Hamidrash Hagodel, where we go to synagogue. They have a relief committee that helps immigrant women and children. And she insisted that Mrs. Wolf come for *Shabbos* dinner tonight. It will be bedlam with all those babies. Mama is now talking about if we get more orders we could send over some of the dresses for Mrs. Wolf to do the finish work on. Things like the buttons and trim, which are hand sewn and do not require a machine. Tovah told me tonight that Mr. Wolf is not the first immigrant husband to simply disappear. It is funny, if this had happened in Russia we would immediately think the man had been killed by ruffians or drafted by the Tsar, or for that matter murdered by the Tsar's soldiers. Here that never crossed anyone's mind. Everyone is quite sure Mr. Wolf is not dead. He has just simply gone.

I wish he would come back. I feel so bad for Blu.

November 29, 1903

Sean O'Malley came after *Shabbos* to put out the lights for us, and after the Wolfs left, Miriam took him aside and told him about how Mr. Wolf had disappeared. She thinks he might be able to help because of all his connections with the fire and police departments. His connections are real, I think, unlike Yitzy's. He met Mr. Roosevelt, the President. Once Mr. Roosevelt was head of the police board in New York. Sean has lots of stories about Theodore Roosevelt. So does Uncle Moishe, for that matter. He made Roosevelt's cavalry uniform for the Spanish-American War.

Well, Bully! That's one of Theodore Roosevelt's favorite expressions, according to Uncle Moishe. He said he felt just "Bully" when he came back from the

Spanish-American War and charged up San Juan Hill. There is no translating it into Yiddish.

So Bully and good night.

December 3, 1903

Writing in English a little bit more. I like third grade a lot. The teacher likes Blu and me. She gives us small poems to read and copy. It is a nice way to learn English. We read and copy one today by Henry Wadsworth Longfellow. The name of the poem is "The Tide Rises, the Tide Falls." It is written in my favorite tense — present. All the words are short. Here are the first two lines: "The tide rises, the tide falls, the twilight darkens, the curlew calls."

The father of Blu is still not here.

December 6, 1903

I read this in newspaper today. It says President Roosevelt has made an island in Florida a sanctuary for sea birds. It is called Florida Pelican Island. I read this to Mama as we sew and she says they treat birds here better than people. She is mad that Beth Hamidrash does not give more money to Mrs. Wolf. Only eight more days until Hanukkah! *It is cold. There are snow flurries. I like the English word "flurries." It means snowflakes with wind. Little snowflakes, I think. Is not my English improving?*

Bon nuit (that is French for good night. I learned it from Mandy).

December 7, 1903

I am so mad at Mama and Papa. They do not let me go to the dancing academies with Tovah and Miriam. Papa had a hard enough time convincing Mama it was all right for Tovah and Miriam. Now Papa and Mama say I am too young. Tovah and Miriam go with Mandy and they learn how to do dances and it is so much fun, says Miriam. Miriam tries to teach me here in the apartment. She speaks just like the dancing master must speak. She says, "One-two three, ladies to the left, gents to the right." She is the gent, I am the lady, and she shows me the steps. It is not the same fun. I want to go. Mama and Papa say not until I am fifteen. That is two years and six months. Only seven more days until Hanukkah. *Hooray.*

Oy, I am so excited that I must write in Yiddish. It would be like stuffing the world into a thimble to have to say in English all this excitement. When I am crossing Ludlow Street today, near the soda shop where Blu and I go, I see a sign. It says that the newly formed Russian Symphony Society of New York is dedicated to the "mission of acquainting the American Public with the works of Russian composers." That there will be a concert given on January 7, 1904, and that they still need musicians. So, I think, Papa! Papa must join this group. Yitzy and Blu are with me. So Yitzy says, "Go sign him up." I say, "Yitzy, how can I? I am just a little kid. I cannot go and sign up Papa." Yitzy turns his palms toward the sky, rolls his eyes, and mutters a real Tanta Fruma: "Even a shelled egg won't fall into your mouth by itself." I look at Blu. She says nothing. Her face is very solemn. But I can see what she is thinking. Do it, don't let your father get so desperate that he leaves like mine. And then I think of another Tanta Fruma: "Words are silver, but silence is golden." My friends have given me both. I am rich!

We all go together to the office of the Russian Symphony Society. It is way over on Second Avenue and

10th Street. I have never been over there before. It is the Yiddish theater district and it looks very exciting. Anyhow, we go into a building, up these rickety stairs, but I hear loud voices at the top and I hear string instruments being tuned. The three of us walk inside and there are all these men and some are jabbering away in Yiddish but most in Russian. I make a quick decision. I must speak Russian, but my Russian is rusty. So when the man behind the desk asked me what I wanted, my tongue stuck to the roof of my mouth. It must have taken a full minute for the Russian words to float down from my brain through the forest of English words and Yiddish ones to get to my tongue, but finally I said it: "I am here for my father. He is a violinist. He is a graduate of the Imperial Conservatory in St. Petersburg and he was a teacher there also for many years." It was like magic. The man's bushy eyebrows went up and the talk in the room died down.

"And what might be your father's name?" he asked. I start to say Yekl, his Yiddish name, but I stop just in time and give his Russian name: "Yasha Feldman."

"Yasha Feldman!" several men exclaim. "He's here?" They get all excited and then one says, "Ahh, no problem then with the Tchaikovsky or the Glinka, if we can get Feldman." And then the man from behind the desk says, "Where can we find him?" "Number fourteen Orchard Street," I say. "Top floor." And I am so happy they did not ask me to fetch him. The Russian Symphony Society is coming to fetch Papa. That is the only way it will work.

When we leave the building Yitzy for the first time in his life is impressed by me and my Russian. "You speak like a White Russian, Zippy. A White Russian *shiksa*. You speak like the Tsarina, Zippy." The very idea! I blast him with my best Yiddish curse: "*Finster zol dir vern*! A darkness should be yours." My tongue should drop out if I speak like that murderer's wife, the Tsarina!

So now tomorrow the Russian Symphony Society comes to call at 14 Orchard Street. I shall tell no one. It shall be a surprise. Oh, *Got-tenyu*! Dear God! That it should all work out. I should be the happiest girl on the Lower East Side!

P.S. Have I mentioned that I have not yet heard from Marie Curie? Mandy helped me mail the letter. But I imagine it takes a long time for a letter to get all the way to Paris, France.

December 11, 1903

They came! They came! They came! The Russian Symphony Society came up all three flights of stairs right into our own apartment on Orchard Street. Oh, and the Uppermost was looking down on us for Reb Simcha wasn't there to smell the place up. Papa's mouth dropped open when the man from the desk walked through the door. "Modeste!" he cried. "Modeste Altshuler!" "Yasha!" the man replied. They had known each other back in St. Petersburg. It was all settled in minutes. Rehearsals begin this Sunday. Mr. Altshuler asked Papa about rehearsing on Saturday but Mama shot him a dark look. Many of the musicians are not observant Jews and do practice on Saturday. Papa said he would come and listen but not play. Mr. Altshuler said that would be good.

Before I went to sleep Papa came in and kissed me and called me his pet name for me, his little *bulbe malakh*. He used to call me *bubeleh*. But I did not like being called a little doll. I said I would rather be called a potato than a silly little doll. "A potato!" he said. "We'll make a compromise: a little bit of earth and a little bit of heaven. You are my *bulbe malakh*, my little potato angel. My *naches*, my special joy." He is very happy. I am very happy.

December 12, 1903

Mama just lit the *havdalah* candle, which signals the end of *Shabbos*. But what a *Shabbos*! I went with Papa right after morning services at the synagogue over to Second Avenue and 10th Street. All afternoon we listened to the orchestra practice. Papa saw some old friends from St. Petersburg. I could tell that although Papa was not actually playing he was taking in every single note. I watched the fingers of his hand press up and down on his thigh as he sat. It was just as if his thigh had strings.

I love that part of the Lower East Side. There are cafés and theaters. I said to Papa that I would love to see a play sometime. We stopped in front of one theater with a colorful poster for a play called *Shulamith*.

December 14, 1903

It is the first night of *Hanukkah* — moonless. There is never any moon on the first nights of *Hanukkah* for it comes on the twenty-fifth day of *Kislev*, when on the Hebrew lunar calendar the moon has vanished. But the holiday is all about light, a gathering of light, and we put our menorah in the parlor window so passersby can see. Miriam and Tovah are already in bed. Miriam keeps asking me when I am coming to bed. But I like sitting right by the window where the single *Hanukkah* light burns. It is bitter cold outside and there are frost trees on the window. They are illuminated by the single candle. The frost trees create on our very own window a miniature forest. If I draw my face very close to the window I can lose myself in this forest. I can imagine the thick forests surrounding our old village of Zarichka. I could perhaps in a moment of *Hanukkah* magic be shrunk to a few inches and step into this miniature forest and be back in Zarichka. It would be a miracle but *Hanukkah* is the time for miracles.

P.S. Still no word from Marie Curie. She must be busy with being so famous because of the award.

December 16, 1903

It is the third night. Three candles glow. I like that word, "glow." I look it up in my dictionary. The candles' small flames light the frost tree forest. I think of Judah Maccabee and his soldiers hiding in the trees of the Judean hills as they plan to attack the Greeks who dirtied the temple. Mama comes to sit by me and watch the forest. Miriam asks when we go to sleep. Mama tells her to hush — she wants to hear about my magic forest. My English is not good enough for me to explain here what I tell Mama about the magic forest. Just little stories. But she laughs. Mama asks me what I shall spend my Hanukkah gelt *on. I say I do not know. I do not tell her I want to save to go to the Yiddish theater and see the play* Shulamith.

December 19, 1903

A forest of candles and a forest of frost trees now blaze in our window on this, the sixth night of *Hanukkah*. Mama has taken to joining me each night at the window. We talk about the magic forest in the increasing light of our menorah. I know now that Mama would never marry Reb Simcha in a thousand years. She is too smart. He might be a *gaon*, gifted in the Talmud learning, but Mama is more than that. When I told her that I could imagine Judah Maccabee hiding out from the Greeks in our magic forest she told me that people when they celebrate this holiday must remember that the battle was a victory of freedom and not triumph. It was a victory of few against many.

I think maybe I understand better why Mama does not want to give up her wig. In a way the Americans are like the Greeks. Oh, they do not force pigs on our altars, of course, but it was very easy for those Jews of ancient times to take up Greek styles in small ways. It is so easy to become like all the others. So hard to stand apart and feel free, feel chosen as Mama says but not superior.

P.S. Two nights during *Hanukkah* I woke in the middle of the night when Miriam came back to bed from visiting the lavatory, and I could feel she was so cold. Something funny is going on. I think she goes outside but I cannot figure out why.

December 20, 1903

Have you ever heard of the Wright brothers? Well, I hadn't either. But I have now! Mandy brought over *The New York Times* and some other papers and there were pictures of the Wright brothers, Orville and Wilbur, and their wonderful flying machine. They call it an airplane. On December 17, on the third day of *Hanukkah*, as it happened, they flew the machine almost 120 feet in 12 seconds. They actually made four flights on that day at a place called Kitty Hawk. The longest flight was 852 feet and took 59 seconds.

Imagine that! I think I want to learn how to fly an

airplane. I think I might want to do that more than be a famous scientist like Marie Curie, who still hasn't written. I made Tovah go up to the roof with me even though it was freezing cold. I just wanted to be up high. It was thrilling for the night was so clear and starry.

Hanukkah is about miracles. Is it so extraordinary that miracles can still happen? And that in 1903 in America during the days of the festival of lights this miracle of the two brothers and their flying machine has happened? I do not know if Mama would look at this as a miracle or not. But I am cutting out pictures of the Wright brothers and taping them to the wall over our bed. I wonder if they are Jewish. I don't think so.

December 21, 1903

Last night of *Hanukkah*. I cannot believe it. You'll never guess what Papa gave me! Tickets to the play *Shulamith*. We go on January 1, a week before Papa's concert. His rehearsing is going well. They are doing some Tchaikovsky, and some Glinka, but most exciting of all some Stravinsky. Papa says New Yorkers will not know what has hit their ears when they hear Stravinsky.

December 23, 1903

I am very worried about Blu and her schoolwork. You see, the teacher says that I am doing excellently. I get 100 percent on all my spelling tests. And I do well in recitation, especially when we have to memorize poems. I like poetry and find it an easy way to learn English, but Blu is not doing so well. It is so hard for her at home helping her mother with all the babies. She has no time to study. I don't know what will happen when the new baby comes. The problem is that the teacher says she is sure I shall be able to move on to the fourth grade within a month. But if Blu can't go with me it will be awful. Poor Blu. Eighty years of blackness upon that no-good father of hers.

December 24, 1903

Tomorrow is Christmas. So no school today or tomorrow or next week. Sean O'Malley came and took Miriam and me uptown to Herald Square to Macy's department store. I could not believe the window decorations. Beautiful silver sleighs drawn by mechanical reindeer and snow-crusted trees sparkling with lights. And then — I think I should try to write this in English for it was so American. *We walked east on 42nd Street and went into Child's Restaurant. And we really did sit down and Sean bought us a treat. I was scared to eat. I mean, it certainly wasn't kosher and what about Typhoid Mary? But Miriam said don't be a ninny,* schmendrik, *the Yiddish sounds better I think. She said you do not have to order pork. Just have some tea and a biscuit. So I order what Miriam orders. I watched how Miriam pours the tea from the little pot into a cup, not a glass the way we always drink it at home and did in Russia. I watch the way she stirs the sugar that is not in lumps but loose as for baking. At home we always put the sugar cube in our mouth while we drink the tea. I watch all this and I think she does this well. She knows what she is doing. She has done this before. She has done this with Sean. And suddenly I know why Miriam sometimes feels cold in bed. She has been out on the roof with Sean — not drinking tea. But other times they go to places like Child's and drink tea. I think maybe I am not a greenhorn anymore. I drink tea in an American restaurant and eat a biscuit and I sit there very calmly and I know that my sister loves a* goy, *a non-Jewish boy, an Irish-American fireman, and I do not faint and I do not have heart blast or whatever they call it when people's hearts stop and they fall dead, and I do not scream. I look very calm, but I cannot believe what I now know for sure.*

December 25, 1903

Back to Yiddish. I think that was pretty good that I wrote all that heart-stopping news in English. I think if I can write English under such nervous conditions I am really making progress. I think of nothing else but Miriam and Sean. It is scary. What if Mama and Papa find out? Mama would die. I wonder if Tovah knows? I do like Sean a lot and I forgot to mention that on our way back downtown he bought me a newspaper because he knows how crazy I am about the Wright brothers, and there were some really good pictures of them for me to cut out. I already have four pictures of the *Wright Flyer,* as their plane is called, on the wall. Which brother is most handsome? Good question. I'm not sure. One has a mustache. One doesn't.

Must go, only ten minutes to *licht bentschen.*

December 29, 1903

I have been going every day throughout school vacation with Papa to rehearsal. It is so much fun. We often go afterward to a café with the other musicians. We drink tea. They serve it Russian style with the glass and the sugar cube. It makes me think of drinking tea with Miriam and Sean. She came to bed cold last night. I feel very uncomfortable being the only one in our family who knows about their secret. I am sure Tovah doesn't know. Tovah sleeps like a bear in the long Russian winter.

January 2, 1904

There is no other choice! I must be an actress. I feel a little bad when I say this but forget Marie Curie, forget Orville and Wilbur. I know my true calling now — acting. Last night we went to the Eden theater and saw *Shulamith*. *Oy, Gotenyu*, Oh, dear God! How else can I describe my feelings? What a story and there is a part for me. One of the children who gets killed. I should be so lucky to die onstage. The play, *Shulamith*, or *The Daughter of Zion*, is set in ancient Judea and it is the most wonderful love story. I cried my heart out. I cried my guts out.

I would not mind discovering radium and pluto-nium. I would not mind flying a flying machine. But it would be settling for me. It would be a second choice.

Papa says he will try and get me pictures of some of the stars, like Sigmund Mogulesko and Bessie Thomashefsky, for my wall. He says the greatest actress of the Yiddish theater is Esther Rachel Kaminska, but she is still in Poland. Oh, well. I will go to more theater here. Papa promises. Meanwhile only six days until the big first concert of the Russian Symphony Society. It is to be at Cooper Union. New York get ready. Here comes Stravinsky!

January 4, 1904

It was a beautiful sunny day today. It feels like spring in the middle of winter. But this confuses because it is like a little joke when you know so much more cold and winter is to come. You cannot get too full of hope. But Yitzy and Blu and I go to our favorite soda shop on Ludlow Street and we take our soda to the curb and sit in the sunshine. The streets run with water. We even take off our shawls and waist jackets. We see children. Little girls do the hopping game over puddles. We each are very quiet. Then suddenly Yitzy says to me, nodding toward the children hopping puddles, "What do you see there?" "I see kids," I say. "I see customers," Yitzy answers. I do not know what he is talking about and Blu does not either. "Customers?" we both say. "Little customers," he replies. I must explain now in Yiddish.

So, Yitzy points out how most all the women and children wear shawls not cloaks. Uptown, he says women of fashion and more well-to-do women wear cloaks. Cloaks are really more practical. They can have pockets and you do not have to hold them on with your hands. They can be lined and warmer. "But we're not uptown," says Blu. "Nobody has enough money here." "But supposing we make a cheaper version that people can afford. Nobody has ever thought of cloaks for little girls. Think how much easier it would be to wear a cloak and play in a cloak rather than a shawl?" I immediately see Yitzy's point. Yitzy says he is going to get his father who is a good designer to design a few cloaks, some for little girls, some for grown-up ladies. All looking very stylish but not costing much money. He then asks if my mother will make up the samples. I think it is really a good idea. So I say I'll talk to Mama about it.

That's all for now in English or Yiddish. I have many long division problems and I am going to try and memorize Mr. Henry Wadsworth Longfellow's poem about the Midnight Ride of Paul Revere. Maybe if I recite this poem good I can ride to fourth grade. Ha ha. I must be getting better with English if I make word-joke like that.

January 5, 1904

Mama likes idea of making samples for Mr. Silver's designs. Two more days until concert. I cannot wait.

January 6, 1904

I cannot believe it but I heard it when I was out in the hall, coming across the air shaft. And I understood almost everything. Finally, Mrs. Sheehan spoke up to the grouchy old lady. She said very clearly, "I am not a sneaky Protestant. I am as Catholic as you are. And if you don't shut that ugly face of yours I am going to go to the priest and tell him . . ." Unfortunately I did not understand what Mrs. Sheehan was going to tell the priest. It must be something bad that the old lady did. Hooray for Mrs. Sheehan.

January 8, 1904

The concert was wonderful. It was held at Cooper Union at Astor Place, in the Great Hall, and there were some real uptown people there! Women in cloaks, not just shawls. Yitzy's right. But most important Papa played magnificently. He played the brand-new Sibelius *Concerto in D Minor* "to perfection." That is what I heard a man near me say. They want Papa to play in more concerts. Just imagine if Papa could give up his job in the shop and teach violin and play in an orchestra all the time. Mama was happy, too. But she did look odd. I do not think there was one other lady there in a wig. They were all so fashionable. Mama was studying their cloaks. The lady sitting in front of us had one with a very stylish stand-out collar, and Mama said she saw how it was faced on the inside and she will tell Mr. Silver about it for his designs.

January 9, 1904

What a day! As if there was not enough excitement last night with the concert. We were all sound asleep when there came a loud knocking at our door. It was Blu. Her mother's time had come. We were all in a flurry for

Mama had promised to go help. Papa was sent to fetch a midwife. In all the excitement no one noticed that Miriam was not there. But then Miriam comes in and she is wearing her heaviest shawl. It is obvious that she has not come in from the lavatory, but no one notices. Except me. So I whisper to her, "Miriam, you better be more careful sneaking around with Sean." Her face froze. So that's how I finally told her I knew! Just popped out. Like Mrs. Wolf's baby. A little girl. So beautiful. Fat and not so red like some, nor so wrinkled.

Half an hour to *licht bentschen*. But we are all so tired that all we are having is soup and potato kugel for *Shabbos* supper. No time to prepare more.

January 12, 1904

Mama has begun on the first samples for Yitzy's father. I help with the cutting. Yitzy helps with the talking. He is going to drive me crazy. He talks all the time about uptown styles he sees. He talks about where to find facing for stand-out collar Mama saw at concert. You would think he is Mr. Macy Department Store. I go to Blu's every day since she has to miss school to help with new baby. I show her schoolwork. I try to help her. But she is falling behind. She don't understand the long division. She cannot read at all the

story we are on in the primer. I write words in big block let-
ters she needs to know and tape them to headboard of her
bed so she sees them when she wakes up and goes to sleep,
but her little brother tears the paper down. Oh dear. I worry.

January 14, 1904

Finally, I really talked to Miriam about Sean. She started crying and says that she is so in love. They want to get married! I gasped when she told me this. She said, "But I am almost sixteen now." She says back in Zarichka the matchmaker would have already found a husband for her. The *shadchen* would have found a Jewish one, I point out. Tovah doesn't know. I can't believe that I know something Tovah doesn't know. But this is all very confusing. I don't want Miriam to get married. It will upset Mama and Papa so much and just when things are going so well. Mama has her dressmaking and Papa is playing his violin again.

January 17, 1904

The weather has turned freezing cold again. Tonight when I went to bed I noticed this beautiful light coming through the window in the parlor. I could not imagine what it was. And then I saw. It was moonlight wrapped around icicles. Tomorrow I go with Mama uptown to deliver the rest of the uniforms for the staff of the lady. The governess delivered the first bunch but the lady is so pleased she wants Mama to come herself and take measurements for a dress for her. This is all working out so well.

January 19, 1904

Well, I never! We went uptown. The Meyers' house is on West 45th Street just off Fifth Avenue. First we were led into a reception hall. There was a tree, would you believe it, in the reception hall? A living, growing tree. Miss Caroline, the governess, said it was a palm tree and that they grow in Florida — where President Roosevelt is protecting the birds. Every surface of every wall was covered with something fancy. Sometimes a tapestry with a picture of unicorns or half-naked people, gods and goddesses, I think, from mythology. And every window had fancy curtains with fringe and swags. And then there were pedestals with marble sculptures of men's heads, no ladies. Mrs. Meyer's boudoir, where Mama made the measurements, looked like a forest of roses. Everything in shades of rose or pink or red. And roses in vases and on cushions and little naked angels, the kind they call cupids, flying around in paintings or carved into the molding of the ceiling. I thought it was a little strange because in each corner of the room there was a cupid perched, but just his head and wings. It was like they had been chopped by a guillotine, the way they did in the French Revolution. Chopped-up angels are not my idea of beauty.

I could not believe it when Mama told me that the Meyers are Jewish. She says they are German Jews and that is different. But Blu Wolf is a German Jew and she is not this way.

Mrs. Meyer was very nice, but I hated the two daughters, Flora and Rosellen. They were very snobby and stuck up. Miss Caroline asked them to entertain me in the music room. So they took me there but they just lounged on these puffy chairs and I had to sit on a hard one, and then they talked in very fast English. I know they did this on purpose. I went over to the piano and I saw music for a piano concerto, Schumann in A Minor. So I said, "I know this piece. My father has played the violin part in it." When I speak they snicker behind their hands at my English. And then they each pick up books and read and do not pay one bit of attention to me.

January 24, 1904

Papa starts Sunday rehearsals again. I love to go with him because he rehearses in the building right next to the theater where we saw Shulamith. Tovah and Mandy and a friend of Mandy's named Mamie came. Mamie is so nice and very pretty. I tell her that I love the Yiddish theater. She says she knows people who work there and will take me over sometime.

January 26, 1904

Guess what? Mamie comes looking for me after school. She says can I come quick with her. There is a rehearsal for a new play. I can come and watch. This is the most exciting day of my life. We sit in the dark theater. Only few people. We see the great actors in their street clothes walking around onstage with their pages of script in hand. I love this. Mamie introduces me to her friend. He is boyfriend, I think, and he works backstage. He is very nice. His name is Boris. He says any time I want to come I just come over. If I am quiet like a mouse no problem.

I think I should probably be writing you in English, because my teacher says I am really progressing. But she does not know that when I really feel something strongly there is only one language for me — Yiddish. This is what I feel so strongly about. The theater. Mamie has taken me twice now to the Eden theater, and I get to watch all the rehearsals. The play they are rehearsing is *Mirele Efros*, or *Queen Lear*. Mandy tells me it is fashioned after none other than Mr. William Shakespeare's *King Lear*, but is actually a better story. Mamie is so lovely. She is two years older than Tovah, nineteen. She is so pretty. She has this pouffy reddish-blond hair and dark eyes and her face looks so delicate. And I love the way Mamie ties her scarf. Not all tightly wrapped like the women in the *shtetl*. No, she does this beautiful thing where it looks like a picture frame around her face. She is going to show me how to do it. She has so much style, Mamie does! She works, like Tovah, in a shirtwaist factory. It is called the Diamond Factory. She is a finisher. She is a member of Yiddishe Yugend. That is how she knows Tovah. But she does not seem as serious as Tovah. And you know she fixes herself up a bit. Tovah never does that. She never fluffs her hair. And she never puts on rouge, which I am sure Mamie does. Oh, well.

February 8, 1904

Guess what? Mamie knows about Miriam and Sean. She says Tovah knows about them now, but was thinking I do not know. I tell Mamie: "Tell Tovah I know." I might be twelve but I know. So there. I think I might as well tell Tovah myself.

February 9, 1904

Tovah knows I know. She is very surprised I know this for so long time, longer than she knows it. We worry together about Miriam now. Miriam needs all the people to worry about her. You can never have enough people to worry about you if you are a Jewish girl in love with a gentile fellow. This can be a very big problem. We all like Sean, at least Tovah and I do. But this is big trouble. That is all I can say. There is not enough English to say all these troubles that they might have.

February 10, 1904

Things are happening fast. Not enough that I have this crazy *meshuggeneh* sister in love with an Irish fireman. Not enough that I am trying to get promoted to fourth grade. Not enough that Papa is rehearsing Rachmaninoff — Mandy calls Rachmaninoff the Grand Canyon of musical compositions, especially the Rachmaninoff number 3. Okay, not enough that Mama is making up all these samples for Yitzy's dream customers! Now, I tell you what Tovah has to go and do: Organize a union!!! She is going to be in big trouble. This could be bigger trouble than a Jewish girl in love with a gentile. This is bigger than the Rachmaninoff number 3! THIS IS BIG TROUBLE!!

So long, *auf Wiedersehen* (German), *zay gezeunt* (Yiddish) *da's viedanyiev* (Russian).

P.S. War between Japan and Russia broke out the day before yesterday. Just thought I'd mention it!

February 12, 1904

Papa brought home two newspapers, the *Jewish Daily Forward* and *The New York Times,* and I was able to translate the *Times* and fill in with the *Forward* the war news. Japanese naval forces attacked Port Arthur in southern Manchuria, which is in China, and they bottled up the Russian ships. It is the first war with something called land mines, which are things that explode out of the ground and kill people by the dozens, and torpedoes, which whiz through the air and also kill people by the dozens. Isn't this amazing all the ways people can think of to kill people? *Oy gevalt.*

February 14, 1904

There is this wonderful holiday here in America. It is called St. Valentine's Day. It is all about love. So guess what? Oh, this is so romantic. Sean gave Miriam a beautiful heart-shaped card. It was edged with lace and had flowers printed on it and a beautiful girl in a swing. And the paper was scented with perfume. Miriam, of course, had to hide it in case Mama finds out. But she told me where she hid it and said it would be fine for me to take it out and look at it anytime Mama wasn't around. So happy St. Valentine's Day.

How could two sisters be so different from one another than Miriam and Tovah? On the very day that Miriam was blushing from her hairline to her collar over the valentine that Sean gave her, Tovah was organizing a cloth workers' union for women in the needle trade. She and her friend Bessie and another girl went over to the United Cloth Hat and Cap Makers' Union and told the boss that they would like to form a women's union. The boss told them that they needed twenty-five other women from many different factories before they could be given a charter and become an official union. Tovah wants to force the management of the factory where she works to treat the women at least as good as the men. Women have to wait longer on payday and their toilets stink. So it is mostly money and toilets. Mama is furious. She said unions are for men not women. A woman who joins a union will never get married. She then said a favorite Tanta Fruma: "Better to be a wise person in hell than a fool in paradise." I guess paradise is supposed to be the union and hell is the shirtwaist factory where Tovah works. Then they trade Tanta Frumas for a while.

Tovah: A boil is fine as long as it's under someone else's arm.

Mama: The chicken who sticks its neck out gets its head chopped off.

Tovah: God loves the poor and helps the rich — that's why we have to get our own union.

Mama: The poor and the rich in the bath are both equal.

I have nothing to add to this conversation.

February 22, 1904

Guess what? Tovah has her union. She and Bessie got all the signatures. They call their union the Working Woman's Circle. Tovah is the president. Who else?

February 25, 1904

Guess what? I got promoted. I am officially a fourth grader now. Teacher is not sure about Blu. She must think about it. But I am so excited I cannot tell you. When you are a fourth grader you learn many more poems and you get to copy in your copy book parts of important American historical writings such as Abraham Lincoln's Gettysburg Address and the Bill of Rights and the Declaration of Independence. I won't be a greenhorn no (any?) more. I am becoming a true

Yankee. I am going to write much more in English now.

Blu is not going to be promoted. This is so sad for me. What will I do without Blu? What will Blu do without me? I went to Teacher and begged after school. I said I would help Blu and so would our friend Yitzy who is very smart. Teacher was very cold to me. She says, "This is not your bizzniss, Zipporah. This is not a decision for a child." This makes me very angry when grown-up people talk this way to me. Children are not too young to work long hours in the shops. Children are not too young to be left on purpose by their fathers as Blu and her sisters and brothers were. I start to explain to Teacher about Blu's father and how much work she has at home now, but Teacher turns her back and begins writing next week's spelling words on the blackboard.

This will be the most difficult writing I have so far tried in English. I want to describe Purim. Purim *is a happy holiday. It is a crazy holiday. We Jews are commanded* to be happy on Purim, *that is the main command. But be happy and be tired is what happens for there is much to do, as you will soon see.* Purim *is told about in the Book of Esther. Esther was the queen of Persia. She was married to King Ahasuerus. He did not know she was Jewish. But then something terrible happens. His evil minister Haman tells him all the Jews must be killed, but Mordechai, who is Esther's cousin, finds out. He goes to Esther and says you must tell the King finally that you are a Jew and if he kills all the Jews you will be dead too. No more hiding that you are Jewish. So she does and the King is very surprised but he loves his wife and now knows how evil Haman is and the Jews are saved.*

So that is the story. We celebrate the holiday in many ways and one way is by sending gifts to people in need. So all night before Purim *Mama and Tovah and Miriam and I bake* hamantaschen *cookies stuffed with dried fruits. The cookies are folded into a triangle shape, the shape of Haman's hat. Mama with sugar and water and cinnamon and lemon juice makes sourball candies, too, and dates stuffed with nuts. We make this food to take to the Wolfs for they are one of the needy families we know. Mama says she wishes she could rent a sewing machine for Mrs. Wolf but she can't. We also take cookies and bread to the Sheehans. This is my idea because I always feel so sorry for Mrs. Sheehan. Mr. Sheehan is not very well. You can hear him coughing a lot through the walls at night. And because of this he cannot keep a job.*

Mrs. Sheehan says thank you for the food. The old lady grumbles something and I see her ugly yellow tooth. Okay, that is all I can write now. I have many more thoughts on Purim. *I don't know if I shall be able to write it all in English however.*

Later the same evening

I must finish about *Purim* in Yiddish for I have many complicated thoughts and we did so much. We got up very early the next morning, the first day of *Purim* to go to the six o'clock service at the synagogue when they read the *Megillah*, the Book of Esther. Mama and Papa had a little tiff. So last night in bed I am thinking about the meaning of the story of Esther. I have so many thoughts, I cannot sleep. I want to talk to someone. Miriam has sneaked out. So I say, "Tovah, you awake?" No answer. So I ask her again. "I am now," she says very grumpy. "What is it?" "Do you think

Esther is like a German Jew?" "What are you talking about?" "I mean she is sort of uptown, you know?" "What?" I start to explain but then I hear Tovah snoring. I start thinking about Mama and Esther, too. Mama is so frightened of losing her Jewishness. She would stay a greenhorn forever if it meant she could be the same Jew she always has been: wig firmly on head, observing every holiday just as she has since she was a little girl. I think about Mama's wigged head. Then I think about Queen Esther who did not even admit to being a Jew but look how she helped the Jews in the end. What a champ! So you can't always tell who is the faithful and who is not despite their wigs and sidelocks.

P.S. I forgot to tell you Miriam and Mandy and Tovah and me and Mamie and Boris all dressed up in costumes for the celebration at the synagogue. Masquerading is part of the holiday. We went as barnyard animals — no pigs, but cows and chickens and billy goats. Then after the synagogue party they were going to go to a café near the Yiddish theaters for more celebration and guess what? Mama let me go with them! I felt very grown-up. I drank Viennese coffee with lots of whipped cream.

March 9, 1904

I am sorry it is so long since I write, no wrote to you. But I am very busy with fourth grade, and now I go to Blu's often to help her with her schoolwork and show her what fourth graders do. She tries some of this work. It is hard for her. One thing we do that she likes is that we try to translate letters from the "Bintel Brief" column of the Jewish Daily Forward. *They are very interesting. There was one today about a lady who came here from Russia to join her husband and found out that he had married another woman. We learned a new word: "bigamist." It means married to more than one woman at a time. It is illegal. The man is now in jail.*

March 10, 1904

Went to the Eden Theater today. I watch them rehearse a play with Sigmund Mogulesko called The Immigrant. *It is wonderful. Mogulesko is a genius actor. Boris says if I come tomorrow after school he will take me to another theater where he works and I can see the world-famous actor Jacob Adler in a production of* Merchant of Venice *by none other than William Shakespeare, in Yiddish. I love it backstage.*

March 11, 1904

*I forgot to tell you that yesterday Boris said to me,
"Well, Zippy, maybe some play that is coming up
will need children and you can audition." I said, "From
your mouth to God's ears, Boris!" Now I can think of
nothing else. I told Miriam last night in bed my secret
dreams of wanting to be an actress. She squeezed my
hand. It was a squeeze that seemed to say we both have
secret dreams, mine the theater and hers love. Then she
said, "What is it about this country that makes one
dream such big dreams?" I yawned sleepily and said, yes,
I knew what she meant and look at Tovah with her union
dreams. There is something in the air here in America that
does this to people.*

March 12, 1904

I know I promised to write in English but this is just too
exciting and I could never express it in English. I must
be writing Yiddish now or I shall pop from all my emo-
tions. Guess what? I went with Boris to the other theater and stood near him in the wings and watched
the great Adler rehearse the role of the Jew Shylock in
The Merchant of Venice. Well, the director said, "Take

five" — that means the actors get a rest period for five minutes. Anyway, Jacob Adler walks off the stage and he passes me, then he pats the top of my head. Jacob Adler the most famous Yiddish actor in the whole wide world pats my head and then he says, "My little bluebird," because you know I have blue eyes — from my father. Then he says, "They are very bright blue eyes. They shine out of the darkness of the wings all the way to the stage. I could see them." Then he walks off. Can you believe it? I can't!

March 14, 1904

I found a picture of Jacob Adler in an old newspaper. It was right behind the pickle shop on Hester Street. It had pickle juice on it, but no matter. I took it home, cut it out, and put it right over the pictures of Madame Curie and the Wright brothers on the wall.

March 15, 1904

Sometimes Tovah really surprises me. I think all she thinks about is her union and organizing the workers and never really notices me, but today she brought me another picture of Jacob Adler that she found in a newspaper. I didn't even think she had noticed the picture I had put up. "How can I not notice?" she said. "His picture is right over our bed!"

March 16, 1904

I am in despair! A play came with parts for children. They needed village children to stone someone to death. So Boris took me over to the theater. And guess what? They say I am too tall. I said I'll shrink. I'll do anything. They don't know that I have a special way of walking, I really do, that makes me look shorter. Why do I have to be so tall? I have grown three inches since coming to America. If I keep up at this rate I shall be seven feet tall by the time I am Tovah's age.

March 31, 1904

It is the first night of Pesach *and as always at the* seder *table we set the wine glass and leave open the door for Elijah, the prophet. But it is not Elijah who walks in. It is Uncle Schmully, Tanta Fruma's husband. He comes to America because he says that the Tsar is drafting men, even older men, into the army for the Russian war with Japan. So now he is here. He looks almost the* same as I remember him from before Tanta Fruma died. He has funny hair. Well, to tell the truth he does not have that much hair. The top of his head is shiny bare. I forget English word for no hair. But around the edges he has puffs of hair that look like smoke. He makes a joke about this. He says, "My head is in the clouds." Uncle Moishe is going to try and get him some work. I don't know where he is going to live. I wish he would live here. He is more fun and smells better than Reb Simcha. Oh, well, I cannot complain. We are lucky, as Papa reminds us. For our last Passover together was three years before and that was when there was the terrible pogrom and the people from Zlinka came to our village and the poor girl with the bandaged head. I still got both my ears! Who cares what Reb Simcha smells like — at least I got a nose to smell him, too!

April 1, 1904

It is the second night of Pesach, the second seder. Uncle Schmully and Uncle Moishe are here again. Uncle Schmully is going to work in the shop where Uncle Moishe used to work before Brooks Brothers. Uncle Moishe brags a lot about the uptown swells that he makes fancy suits for at Brooks Brothers. I start to brag about

Mama making clothes for Mrs. Meyer. She is a fancy up-town swell, too, after all. But Papa makes a dark look. He says uptown swell German Jews are the worst because they don't speak Yiddish and they think all Russian Jews are dirty and it is nothing to brag about. I feel bad. I don't like to upset Papa but I don't think it's right for him to speak harsh to me.

April 2, 1904

I am still upset about Papa talking that way to me. I am upset about many things. I make a list.

1) Papa speaking harshly
2) being too tall to play a child in the play
3) nobody paying attention to me much anymore. Mama is so busy with Mrs. Meyer's order. Miriam is so busy with love and Sean O'Malley. Tovah is busy with the union. Yitzy is busy with his father's samples. Blu is busy with her mother's new baby. I feel alone and left out. Marie Curie never wrote me back. I wrote the Wright brothers, too. They never wrote back either and now I am thinking seri-ously of flying again because I think I never get part in theater, so I wish they would write back. I

have so many newspaper pictures on my wall of them.

That's all. I am tired of writing English.

April 8, 1904

Very good news! Yitzy's father has an order for over two hundred ladies' and children's cloaks from his samples. Now Yitzy is running around looking for space where they can set up to make them, and he is going to need lots of help. I said to Yitzy maybe he would hire my father. And he says, "I have better plans for your father." Guess what Yitzy's plans are? He wants Papa to be the boss of the shop — to do the hiring and organize the work load and get the bundles and distribute them. He says that his father is not organized and that my father would be better at this. I think that this is very interesting but I am not sure. I think my father might have to be convinced.

April 11, 1904

Convinced? Did I say convinced? We have never had such a fight in our family. It makes me tremble to think about it. I told Papa Yitzy's idea and he said no and picked up his violin to start practicing before going to rehearsal for the next concert. Then Mama says, why not, Yekl? It would make good money. Good money is Mama's code for no more boarder, no more Reb Simcha. I am all for that. So then we all start talking. I say it would be great and Tovah and Miriam agree. Suddenly without warning Papa stood up, turning red. Gripping the bow to the violin in his hand he struck the air with it. "You don't learn anything in a sweatshop except being a sweater. You think I came here to learn how to exploit, to be a boss? That is vile. Never! Never!"

Suddenly I think that maybe Papa is the old-fashioned one and Mama the real Yankee. I think Mama would open a sweatshop in a minute. She is sort of running one now to do the work for Mrs. Meyer. I mean she hires Blu's mother and she says if she can get some more orders she will rent a machine for Mrs. Wolf. Oh, but the fight was so horrible.

April 15, 1904

Half an hour until licht bentschen. *Guess what? Uncle Moishe and Uncle Schmully are both going to work part time for Yitzy's father. And Uncle Schmully is going to do the job Yitzy offered Papa. I feel so left out. Why can't Papa do this? Reb Simcha smells worse than ever. I hate him I hate him I hate him and if Papa would take this job we would not have to have Reb Simcha as a boarder.*

April 17, 1904

You cannot imagine what has happened. It is so terrible and I feel so guilty. I am tempted to go back and scratch out my last entry. But I cannot. I must live with this shame. Reb Simcha died last night. What can I do? Nothing, absolutely nothing. Here is how it happened. He was sitting as he always does on the little cot like a pile of — yes — old smelly rags. Mama had just brought him his glass of evening tea, as she always does, and a biscuit. All of a sudden it was as if he had been hit by lightning. He made a quick movement. He became rigid, his eyes locked in fright wide open, and he fell sideways. Mama and I both ran to him. There were crumbs on his beard and a look of outrage in his eyes. I think he was looking right at me. Mama whispered, "I think he is dead." We were home alone as Papa was at a rehearsal. Mama sent me to the synagogue. Two men came back with me. Mama was in a daze. I was in a daze. The men were very businesslike. Soon Reb Simcha was gone from our apartment. It is all so strange. He had no relatives to sit *shiva* so we do now. The mirrors in our house are covered for the period of mourning. We sit on low stools and some boxes. Papa goes to work, but I miss school. Mama said I didn't have to, but I have to. I know I did not cause Reb Simcha's death. I mean, I think I know that, but how could I have had such terrible thoughts about the poor old man right before he died? And all because he was a little bit smelly. I cannot even remember the smell now. It is gone — like Reb Simcha.

Miriam told me that Sean told her that in the Catholic religion one can go and confess their sins and ask forgiveness once a week. I wish Jews had that. I shall have to wait until *Yom Kippur* to be washed of this sin, if I can even then. *Yom Kippur* is five months away! Serves me right, I guess.

April 21, 1904

I went back to school today for the first time since Reb Simcha's death. Guess what? Blu has finally been promoted. She's in fourth grade. But guess what else? I have been promoted to fifth grade. So we're still not together! But Blu was so pleased and grateful to me for my help that she bought me a soda and a pickle after school. She says she will catch up with me before the end of school. We went back to her apartment and did what we most like to do to practice our English. We translate the letters in the Bintel Brief. There was a good one today. A lady wrote in and said her husband does not like that she is going to night high school two days a week. He does not believe she has the right. The Bintel Brief editor wrote back that this is America and everyone has the right to an education whether that person is man or woman. Blu and I say we shall never marry a man like that woman's husband. Of course, I think Blu maybe never will marry after her father goes and disappears.

April 30, 1904

Uncle Schmully is our new boarder. He is fun. He does not seem so old but he must be nearly sixty as Tanta Fruma would be almost sixty if she were alive. Uncle Schmully wants me to teach him English. He will pay me!

Uncle Schmully is a fast learner. In just three days he knows the names of the days of the week. I write down ten vocabulary words every day for him. He learns them fast. He wants to learn words for his work — like needle, scissors, thread, and words for food and buying things in stores.

But of course Tovah has her list of words that she wants to teach Uncle Schmully. Here is part of Tovah's list that she gave me to teach him:

union
organize
oppressed
exploited

I told Tovah if you want him to learn these words, you teach him.

Mamie brought me some more pictures of Jacob Adler and one of his wife, Sarah, in a play called God, Man and Devil. *I want to have a whole wall covered with stars of the Yiddish theater. Boris says he will get me a poster advertising a show.*

May 15, 1904

Uncle Schmully knows how much I love theater and through his work he gets special price for tickets to a play, but not a Yiddish play. Uncle Schmully says he does not want to hear Yiddish. He wants to hear English. So we go to see the new musical on Broadway Piff!! Paff!! Pouf!! *With Eddie Foy. It is very gay and lively. Good music, but I like Yiddish theater better.*

May 18, 1904

No comparison of Broadway theater and Yiddish theater. Last night I saw Jacob Adler in *The Beggar from Odessa*. Papa bought tickets for just him and me. This was good. Because ever since Passover when Papa spoke so sharply to me I've felt very bad. I think Papa noticed this. I think maybe Papa is a little bit jealous of the attention I get from Uncle Schmully. Maybe that is why he did it. Jacob Adler is the most extraordinary actor. He has very large eyes and there is more white to his eyes than the colored part. So when he opens them wide in terror or shock they are hypnotic. Now that is acting. How could I have ever thought of becoming a physicist like Marie Curie or flying an airplane? I must act.

May 19, 1904

I think Mama is up to something. When I came home from school Pesseye, the matchmaker, was here. I think Mama is getting set to marry off either Tovah or Miriam. Why else would a matchmaker come to our house?

Mama has another client now besides Mrs. Meyer. Tomorrow we are taking Mrs. Meyer her order. I am not looking forward to it as I hate those girls. They treat me so terrible. We had to go up for a fitting about three weeks ago and Flora the oldest one said something so nasty about Mama. I overheard her. She called my mother "an Oriental piece of antiquity"! German Jews are really full of themselves. They don't speak Yiddish and anything east of Germany they consider the Orient and a traditional Jewish woman like Mama, well — an antique! Can you imagine? If Mama wants to wear a *sheidel*, it's her business. But, my goodness, if she really does want to use a matchmaker and arrange weddings for us that is our business. Still, she is not an Oriental piece of antiquity.

You will never believe what happened. We went up-town to deliver the summer dresses to Mrs. Meyer and when we got there the butler told us we would have to wait a few minutes as Mrs. Meyer and her daughters were being photographed in the music room. So we waited. I was getting bored and decided to just go have a peek. Well, I nearly screamed, but thank God I did not. Guess who the photographer was? Mr. Wolf, Blu's father. I ran back to tell Mama. She said we must hide. He must not see us. I said, "What? Are you crazy? He should hide." Then Mama says if she sees him she might just kill him. For the next ten minutes until the photography session is over we are in agony. We do not know what to do. We sit there like frozen statues. We see him pass into the hallway and finally I jump up and run out after him right through the front door. He is still on the steps. The butler is helping him and there is a cab waiting. "Mr. Wolf!" I cry. I see his shoulders jerk, but he does not turn around. So I go up to him as he is climbing into the cab. "Mr. Wolf!" I shout and this time tug on his sleeve. He turns around and says, as cool as anything, "I am not Mr. Wolf, young lady. You must be mistaken." Then he climbs into the cab and drives off and I am left shouting right there on 45th Street, "You are Mr. Wolf! And you have a family."

Mama says we must keep this to ourselves. It will only cause pain to Blu and her mother. I don't know whether I can keep this to myself.

May 29, 1904

I cannot help but think about what I saw. Mr. Wolf uptown. It is all I think about. I have not told Blu.

June 5, 1904

For almost a week now I have thought of nothing except Mr. Wolf.

June 6, 1904

Today I decided I must do something about Mr. Wolf, so I wrote a letter to the Bintel Brief in the Jewish Daily Forward *asking them what I should do. I hope they write back, but I don't know. Marie Curie and Orville and*

Wilbur have not acknowledged my existence. Pretty fancy English writing, eh? Everyone says my English is phenomenal (another fancy English word). I think teaching Uncle Schmully has actually helped my English more than anything.

June 10, 1904

I was right. Mama was making business with the matchmaker. The matchmaker came tonight to meet Tovah. Tovah had a fit. But she was very clever about it. She talked about all of her union activities. She talked about emancipation, women's rights, and she talked about money. I watched along with Uncle Schmully (Papa was at a rehearsal) while Mama got redder and redder and the matchmaker's face slowly turned to stone. Finally the matchmaker gets up and says very stiffly, "I have no further business here." Mama crumpled into a heap and cried. None of us knew what to do. Then Uncle Schmully said, first in Yiddish and then in very near perfect English, "Sarah, this is America." Mama just stared at him and then adjusted her wig.

Today was our last day of school before summer vacation and guess what? I have been promoted to seventh grade. Teacher said I could skip sixth grade because sixth is not that different from fifth. But in a little more than a week I turn thirteen so in the fall I will still be a little old for seventh grade. Teacher says if I work hard in the fall I should be able to go on to eighth grade before long. I say, how long? She says oh you know, a few months. I say what is few? Three or four? Maybe she says, maybe just a couple. I say what is couple — two? She nods. She says, "Zipporah, you are always so rushed. What's the big hurry?" What's the big hurry? I want to say. You try being twelve years old and sitting in little chair with kids half your size, you would be in a hurry too. She doesn't know how big a hurry I am in. I will be in seventh grade one month, not two. Then on to eighth grade. Over the summer I shall help Blu. I am going to push, pull, drag her along as fast as I can. She will be in eighth grade with me by Purim at the latest. Just watch.

June 16, 1904

We slept on the roof last night as it was so hot. Sean came by and told us fantastic stories about the World's Fair that just opened in St. Louis. He says there is this new invention called an ice cream cone. I tried to imagine what he describes. He says it is like a biscuit or thin cookie rolled into a horn shape and people put ice cream in it. You lick the ice cream and you bite the cone. It sounds difficult.

June 18, 1904

Papa played in another concert last night. This is the third since January. One piece was the Dvořák Serenade for Strings in E Major. *I heard someone say Papa's little solo in the second movement was "dazzling." I love that word, "dazzling." People have been asking Papa to give lessons. But he hardly has any time. Sometimes before or after a rehearsal he will. We took the Sixth Avenue elevated uptown to where the concert was held. I love riding on the elevated. It is much more fun than the streetcar. You can look right inside people's windows. There is one point at 37th Street where the tracks came so close, I*

could see the food on the family's table. Potatoes on a
platter.

June 22, 1904

Mama has not been feeling well. I think it is the
heat. I hope she is better by tomorrow for it is my birth-
day.

June 23, 1904

Today I am thirteen. But Mama is feeling still bad, so no
lekache. *She makes the best* lekache *for birthdays. Al-*
ways swirls of chocolate and cinnamon and sprinklings
of sugar powder. I feel little bit sorry for myself. Papa
has rehearsal and Tovah has union meeting tonight. Old
Mrs. Sheehan spent forever in the lavatory and I had
to knock to ask her to hurry a bit because Mama was
feeling ill. She came out scowling and said, "She too
good to puke in a bucket?" Such a nice lady, old Mrs.
Sheehan.

Blu says she'll come over if she can get away from
the little kids tonight. Yitzy is now running a machine
in his dad's new business. He works day and night since
school is out. He wants me to come over and pull

threads from the basted hems. Forget it, I say. Not on my
birthday.

June 24, 1904

I must write about my birthday in Yiddish. How could
I have ever imagined how things would turn out? I was
sitting there feeling very sorry for myself when suddenly Mamie and Boris show up. They burst into the
apartment and they have tickets for *Alexander, the
Crown Prince of Jerusalem* with none other than Boris
Thomashefsky who some think is as good as Jacob
Adler, though not me. But the play was wonderful. He
wore tights and played many romantic love scenes with
Sophia Karp, who is beautiful. I've never seen such
scenery. And there is the heat of the lights, and the
sweet oily smell of the greasepaint. I love it. I want to
be a part of this world.

Then we all went over to Second Avenue to the
Café Royale. Tovah and Mandy and Miriam came
along. Sean showed up later and he and Miriam gave
me a set of ribbons for my hair. Tovah gave me a pin-on
lace collar that you can attach to the neckline of any
dress. I put it on right there and tied the ribbons in my
hair and I sipped my coffee and ate a pastry. And I

spoke English and understood all the English that was spoken. Then guess what? Suddenly it seemed as if a forest of flowers was moving toward our table. The forest came right up to me. And then out from behind the bunches of lilies and roses popped a face. Papa's! What a birthday I had! Hair ribbons, greasepaint, flowers, and speaking English like a Yankee! I'm not a greenhorn anymore.

P.S. I had a funny thought. I wonder if Papa noticed that Sean and Miriam were sitting side by side at the Café Royale? Their shoulders had been touching when Papa arrived and I know for a fact they were holding hands under the table. I peeked.

June 30, 1904

Papa is so busy with rehearsals for the Fourth of July concert. They are playing the Dvořák New World Symphony. I go with him to rehearsals whenever I can. It is the most exciting music ever. Dvořák wrote this as a kind of musical letter to his friends back in Europe to tell them about America when he came here ten years or so ago. It has bits of Negro spirituals and American folk music. There are parts that rumble and

pound like mighty rivers and other parts so delicate and
fine.

July 1, 1904

Must write in Yiddish. I'm so excited. My letter about
Mr. Wolf was printed along with an answer in today's
Bintel Brief of the *Jewish Daily Forward.*

I wrote the whole story of Mr. Wolf up to when I
saw him uptown. Then I said I have not the heart to tell
my dear friend that I have seen her treacherous father,
yet it eats at me day and night. What should I do?

Here is the answer:

*We think you have answered your own letter when you
say you have not the heart to tell your friend. What good
would it really do except to cause your friend and her family more pain? This treacherous man has no intention of
coming back to his family. The family, as you say, seems to
be making out as best it can. The wife seems to have put
this behind her and moved on, and so must you.*

July 2, 1904

*From now on I make a promise to write only English. I
do not want to fall behind over the summer. Mama is*

still not feeling well. I wonder what is wrong with her. She often is sick to her stomach in the morning. I went to rehearsal again today. Something exciting happened. An important-looking lady came up and spoke to Papa. He said that she is from the New York National Conservatory of Music. She would like him to be in a special concert. I wish Papa could quit his job and just be a violinist.

July 3, 1904

Guess what? You will never believe this. Blu thinks that her mother and Uncle Schmully are, as the American expression goes, "sweet for each other." For the past month they have both been working for Yitzy's father on the big cloak order. This is really something, isn't it? I am glad I did not tell Blu about her father, but if Uncle Schmully and Mrs. Wolf are really in love how can they get married if Mr. Wolf is still here and alive? Would not Mrs. Wolf be a bigamist? I might have to write the Bintel Brief again.

July 4, 1904

We all went uptown to Carnegie Hall to the concert. It was wonderful and thank goodness Mama is feeling better. Afterward we went to the Central Park and there were fireworks and Papa bought us lemonade. It was so hot when we got home that Tovah and Miriam and even Uncle Schmully slept outside. The night sky was so clear and the stars so beautiful. Little pieces of the Dvořák music kept swirling through my brain as I looked at the night sky. And then I saw a shooting star! And it so reminded me of the quick, lively opening of the New World Symphony. *And I begin to think I am in the New World. It is the Fourth of July, the Day of Independence. These very thoughts make quick little exciting feelings beat in my chest. I cannot sleep, so I get up and walk to the edge of the roof. There is an easy connection to the roof next door. Suddenly I see two figures embracing and kissing so passionately. I know in my heart that it is Miriam and Sean. I am thrilled but I am frightened.*

July 7, 1904

I have a small job but I do not get paid for it. I am working at the Hebrew Immigrant Aid Society making bundles of clothes for new immigrants. So many come in. The pogroms in Russia are worse than ever. People leave by the thousands. So we must all help. Blu by the way, is really catching up. I gave her a book of Longfellow poems that Papa bought for me and she is reading them and under-standing them all. We especially love "The Song of Hi-awatha." When at night I sleep on the roof I whisper these wonderful words that I write here by heart: By the shores of Gitchee Gumee, By the shining Big-Sea-Water, Stood the wigwam of Nokomis, Daughter of the Moon, Nokomis. Dark behind it rose the forest, Rose the black and gloomy pine-trees.

July 10, 1904

I know I promised to write in English but I cannot now. Something extraordinary has happened. Miriam and Sean got married. No one can believe that they would go off and do such a thing. But they did. Mama and Papa are stunned. They walk in a daze. It is unimagin-able that someone in our own family has married a non-Jew. You sometimes hear about this happening to other people but not anyone you really know. Mama is now covering the mirrors. She is drawing out the low stool and the boxes we sat on when Reb Simcha died. Yes, she insists that we sit *shiva* for Miriam and mourn as if she has died. I am not comfortable with this at all. But I cannot explain it. I don't think Papa is either. I do not feel like writing anymore.

July 18, 1904

I have not written for a week. These were seven horrible days. I have come to be angry with Mama. I think sitting shiva *for Miriam is stupid. I do not approve of what Miriam did, but she is not dead. She is in love and although her marrying makes our family unhappy she makes Sean happy, and Sean makes her happy. I cannot pretend she is dead. Mama forbids us to say her name. She says if I meet her in the street I must not speak to her. She tries to make me promise. I would not promise. Papa tries to make Mama not make me promise. Then Mama got mad at both of us. There was a big fight. Papa tries to calm Mama. He says she will hurt herself and make herself sick again. Uncle Schmully too tries to calm Mama but it does not work. I hate Mama's old country ways. I hate her* shtetl, *village ways. I wish she would take off her ugly wig. I wish she would be more American. Her English stinks.*

July 19, 1904

I am getting bored with summer. I wish school would start again. I went to Yitzy's father's place over on 4th Street and pulled basting threads with Blu. We made fifty cents. We went and bought seltzer and knishes and sat and ate them on a corner of Hester Street.

July 22, 1904

This is the second Shabbos *since Miriam got married. I hate* Shabbos *now because of course Sean no longer comes to turn out the lights. And it just reminds me of the way things used to be and never will be again. We have a new* Shabbos goy, *Malachy Sheehan, Mrs. Sheehan's oldest son. He is eight.*

July 23, 1904

Slept on the roof again tonight. The roof is definitely for lovers. Guess who I saw creeping across our roof toward the roof of number 20 Orchard, the Wolfs' building — Uncle Schmully! Blu says she thinks her mother goes somewhere at night when they are all asleep. Well, I could tell her, it's the roof.

July 26, 1904

Now a lot of things start to make sense. I know why Papa is always fussing about, "Sarah, be careful, you don't want to get sick." "Sarah, don't get excited, it's not good for your condition." And now I know why he has been so good about remembering his morning prayers. Mama is going to have a baby. I am not sure how I feel about all this. I am not sure if it's a baby I want. I want my grown-up sister back. I miss her so much. I would miss Tovah too but it is not the same with Tovah. She is so serious and always thinking about her union. Miriam always listened to my dreams about acting. Miriam was not so interested like Tovah in changing the world. Miriam was interested in how an individual person could change. She changed herself. She is a married woman, married to a non-Jew. I want to change myself, too. I want to be an actress. Now how can I talk about that to a baby? You tell me.

August 5, 1904

It has been exactly twenty-seven days since Miriam has run off with Sean. No one has seen her. Tovah said she heard she was living up on 110th Street. I think Tovah knows but is not saying. I think Tovah might have even seen her. I

*miss Miriam more every day. I am not getting used to this.
I don't think Mama misses her at all. To Mama she is dead
and it is a waste of time thinking about or missing a dead
person. Mama talks about the new baby all the time. Does
she really believe she can replace Miriam with the new
baby?*

August 10, 1904

*Twenty-four days until school starts. I can't wait. Twenty-
two days until the first anniversary of our coming to America. I suppose it is another kind of birthday really — the
day we came to America.*

Thirty-two days since Miriam left.

August 12, 1904

*Sometimes people really surprise you. Yitzy for one. I never
think that Yitzy thinks about anything except how to
get ahead — how to get quickest through school, how
to make the most money for his father, how to get this,
how to get that, but guess what? Yitzy bought me tickets
to see* Mirele Efros, *or* Queen Lear. *It stars (I love
that Americans take a noun like "star" and turn it into
a verb!) Keni Liptzen. It was very nice of Yitzy to think*

of me. He says he knows I miss my sister and have been sad.

I had a fight with Tovah last night. I know it was all my fault, but I am not that sorry. I started thinking more and more about how very nice it was of Yitzy to take me to theater, to say how he knows I miss my sister. This started me thinking about Tovah and how she does not seem to miss Miriam and does not care how much I miss her. So I ask Tovah last night when we were out on the roof sleeping. I say, "Tovah, I don't think you think about Miriam. I don't think you miss her. I miss her so much." And she says to me, "I try not to think about things I cannot change." This gets me very angry because I know that she is talking about her union. That is all she ever thinks about. So I blow up. "I am not talking about a union, Tovah," I say. "I am talking about people, individual people — me, Miriam, and how terrible I feel. I am talking about feeling and not thinking. Don't you ever feel, Tovah?" Tovah just got up, picked up her blanket and pillow, and left the roof. She went inside to sleep. I spent the rest of the night crying. I could not even see the stars. They were all smeared because of Tovah. I am so mad at her.

August 15, 1904

First Yitzy surprised me, now guess who? Tovah. Today on our bed I found a little bag of candy and a note in Tovah's crimped-up handwriting. Here is what it says: "Dearest Zippy, I am very sorry. You are right to talk about feeling and not thinking. I often do not know how to sort out my feelings. But I do miss Miriam and I do care that you have such pain over all this. You are better at knowing feelings than I am and because of this I think you will be a great actress. Love, Tovah."

I cried again.

August 18, 1904

You'll never guess what. Yitzy found out where Miriam is living. Through his uptown connections. He asked me if I want to go see her. Isn't it funny, but now I am frightened. This would be the most disobedient thing I have ever done. I must think about it.

August 25, 1904

Every day I think about whether I should go see Miriam. It haunts me. I want to so bad. Blu says I should. She will go with me. I just don't know.

August 26, 1904

I am going to go. I just need to see her even if I don't talk to her. Yitzy says he will take me.

August 27, 1904

I went. We waited forever outside her building. But we did not see her. I was so disappointed I started to cry. Yitzy was so nice. He told me not to cry. We must try again. We must come early in the morning because that is probably when she goes out to do her shopping.

August 28, 1904

Went again. No Miriam.

August 30, 1904

No Miriam. I grow desperate. School starts soon.

September 1, 1904

Saw her!! But then I was so scared I just hid in the shadows of an alley. She looks beautiful but so different. She really does look like a grown-up married lady. And there was something very still about her face. Very calm. I do not think she misses us at all.

I feel even sadder, now, although I know she is all right. I have such an empty spot inside me. And here it is the anniversary of our arrival in America.

September 2, 1904

Saw her again. I went without Yitzy this time. I pulled basting threads to save for the money for the elevated and took it uptown all by myself. Someday I shall get up the nerve to talk to her. But I just want to look at her for now. I followed her to a fruit market on Broadway and 112th. I watched how she spoke with the vendor, a lady. She was lively and charming and I heard the lady say, "And how is Mr. O'Malley?" These words were so unbelievable to my ears. I thought, Can this be my sister? I wonder if she ever thinks of us, of me. I wonder if she remembers that I have a dream, too.

September 6, 1904

Every day for the past five I have seen and followed Miriam and every day it has become harder for me to imagine myself going up and talking to her. Well, today something happened. She saw me. You see, I had been standing behind a cart at the fruit market and the cart suddenly pulled up a few feet. So she could plainly see me. She had just picked up some fruit and she was sniffing it just the same way Mama does. Then she looked up. She looked directly at me and her mouth started to open. But I got so scared. I just turned and ran away. I do not know why I did this. I just knew I couldn't speak to her yet. Now I feel almost ashamed. I don't know why. She must think I am terrible. But then since I have been seeing her these past days she seems so complete, so in a world of her own, I think I must not disturb her. Maybe Mama was right. I should be thinking her dead. But I cannot. And I cannot stop following her. School starts tomorrow. I will not be able to follow her. Besides, it costs too much taking the elevated uptown every day.

September 7, 1904

First day of school. The teacher seems to like me. She made me class monitor. I helped pass out books. I open the windows with the long pole. I wash the blackboard. The teacher likes poetry very much and we get special points for reciting poems. I am going to try and memorize the first portion of "The Song of Hiawatha." In history we shall be learning about the American Revolution and she will give us each a famous patriot to research and write a report on. In arithmetic we are learning about decimal points and percentages. Yitzy knows all about these. He says he shall help me. I noticed today that Mama is getting fat — or at least her stomach is. I try to be excited about the new baby but it is hard.

September 10, 1904

It is Rosh Hashanah. *This makes me miss Miriam more than ever. I remember last year when we went to synagogue and had fits of giggles watching Reb Simcha turn red as a tomato. Now Reb Simcha's dead and Miriam is a married lady uptown. Things change so fast. I never would have dreamed! One thing I did dream of was writing in English — and here I do it.*

September 11, 1904

Mama and Papa had a fight tonight. She thinks he is spending too much time at rehearsals. She says that we will need more money when the new baby comes. She brings up again how she wishes Papa would go and work for Yitzy's father. They keep getting new orders. Yitzy is in high school but often skips to help his father. They are getting rich, Mama says. I look at Mama as she speaks these words. She sits very straight, her stomach beginning to bulge. Papa keeps saying he did not come to America to learn how to be a sweater. Then Mama mutters under her breath a Tanta Fruma: "A strange fool is laughable, but your own fool is shameful." She pulls her wig a bit to set it straight. What a strange woman she is. One part of her is still back in Zarichka, still in the shtetl *with her old ways, and yet another part of her is very American. She wants the money. She wants the promise of this new world. I think maybe in some ways she is less greenhorn than Papa, believe it or not. It makes her very difficult because she wants it both ways.*

September 12, 1904

Remember how I said that Mama wants it both ways? Here is the perfect example. Tovah came home and was talking about a speech former President Grover Cleveland gave, which was reported in the paper. She said he said that "sensible and responsible women do not want to vote." Tovah said, "Now isn't that the stupidest thing you have ever heard?" But Mama shakes her head and says no, Mr. Cleveland is absolutely right. "Is he Jewish?" she asks. "He sounds so smart." Tovah nearly exploded. "Mama!" she screamed. "How can you come to America and think this way? We should have the vote. That is what is sensible." But Mama just shakes her head. See what I mean about Mama: one foot in the shtetl, *one foot in America. She drives us all crazy.*

September 15, 1904

All Tovah talks about is the presidential election to be held in November and how terrible it is that women cannot vote. She is for Alton Parker, the Democratic candidate, and not Teddy Roosevelt, the Republican one. I like Mr. Roosevelt. He's the one who helped the pelicans in Florida. I have pic-

tures of Mr. Roosevelt pinned to the wall. Next to Madame Curie. Papa brought me another one just today. Tovah says the Democratic precinct captain will be coming around to talk to us about Parker and we should at least get down the pictures of Teddy Roosevelt. I guess the precinct captain doesn't know Papa can't vote because he isn't a citizen.

Saw Miriam again today but she didn't see me. It is strange, I don't really have the urge to talk to her now. She seems so different. But I just like to see her and know she is all right. I have thought of telling Tovah, but am afraid. Tovah is so wrapped up with the election and the union.

September 20, 1904

Yom Kippur *was yesterday. These holidays are so hard without Miriam.* Sukkot *will be the worst because I shall remember how Sean helped us build the* sukkah *booth and how we all ate outside and this was before anyone knew or suspected anything about Sean and Miriam. Why did they have to go and ruin it all by falling in love and getting married?*

September 22, 1904

Sukkot *has been better than I thought, mostly because of Uncle Schmully. He is so funny and he is clever and he made us a beautiful* sukkah *this year. He punched designs with a nail in tin cans and then we put candles in them and they shine with the prettiest bits of light on our* sukkah *table. We got the whole thing up and it was quite warm. So Uncle Schmully said he would sit outside on the fire escape in the* sukkah *while he smokes his evening cigar. I don't know what made me do this, but all of a sudden I told Uncle Schmully about my trips uptown to see Miriam and how I was afraid to speak to her. He took my hand and patted it and said, "Don't be afraid, Zipporah. Never be afraid to love." This astonished me. And then I told him how I could not bear that Mama sat* shiva. *That Mama thinks of Miriam as dead and that on* Yom Kippur *I tried to ask God about this. How I felt that even God could never make me understand this. That I say to God, What is right about a woman saying a child is dead when she is not? And that now I feel funny about asking these questions.*

126

This is so exciting. And only fifteen minutes until licht bentschen. *Even so I am going to try to write in English and not Yiddish. Boris took me to the theater today. He was working backstage at the Thalia. And I sat in the wings quietly as I always do when he works and watched the play. It was* Rabbi Akiba and his Twenty-four Thousand Disciples *with Yekl and Minnie Leibowitz. Well, the stage manager says to Boris how the assistant prop girl is always so mixed up and half the time does not show up and that he needs someone else. So Boris looks straight at me and says, "How 'bout it, Zippy? You want to be assistant prop girl? We only play three nights a week — Saturday (after sundown), Sunday, and Thursday." Am I dreaming? From your mouth to God's ears, I am thinking. "Of course!" I say. I thought maybe Mama would say no. But she didn't when she heard that Boris would himself take me home from the theater in the evenings. If there is one good thing that has come out of Miriam marrying Sean it is that nothing seems so bad to Mama by comparison. I begin my job in just a few days. I am so excited I cannot wait.*

September 26, 1904

I think in another week I shall be ready to do my recitation of Hiawatha. I have been thinking that Hiawatha would make a wonderful play in Yiddish. If they make Mr. Shakespeare into Yiddish theater why not Mr. Longfellow? Uncle Schmully is very helpful with arithmetic. He is an expert decimal person and really understands percentages. Yitzy's good, but Yitzy does it all in his head and just keeps saying, "Don't you get it? Don't you get it?" Uncle Schmully, despite his English, which is not nearly as good as Yitzy's, can explain it much better.

September 27, 1904

I am really glad Uncle Schmully has moved in with us. He is the only person who really treats me like an equal, or seems to have any time for me. Papa is always working or rehearsing. Mama just doesn't pay much attention to anything except her work — she has more orders and Tovah is always with the union. Uncle Schmully not only explains decimals but he is telling me how bad things are getting in Russia. Uncle Schmully knows a lot. He was a member of an organization in Russia called the Bund. They met in secret in forests, in farmer's sheds, in tiny villages.

The Tsarist government hated the Bund, but the Bund continued and began printing leaflets talking about human rights and many of the leaders led demonstrations. Soon members were being imprisoned and killed and tortured by the Tsar. The Tsar made harsher and harsher rules and laws. Uncle Schmully says that for the Jewish people in the settlement it is like a hangman's rope tightening around their necks. And then when they want to kill them fast, Uncle Schmully says, they make a pogrom. I asked Uncle Schmully, "Do you think Tsar Nicholas is really evil? Papa says he is just very stupid." And Uncle Schmully says something very interesting: "I think there is a point where stupidity can become evil, and yes, the Tsar reached that point many years ago. He is now evil." I think about that all night long. You see what I mean, Uncle Schmully discusses things with me as an equal.

September 30, 1904

Last night was my first night as prop girl. I got there very early. There are many props that have to be handed to stagehands, or to actors as they come offstage during the performance. They call these props the "handoffs." The handoffs must be very well organized and one must be ready with them. The script was well marked to show me when they were needed. Boris had given me the script before and I studied it very hard. I did my job perfectly! It was so exciting. The actors all complimented me and the stage manager said I was as good as gold!

October 2, 1904

I love my job. Tonight was my third night at the Thalia. I now know all the actors by name. They call me Zippy. Boris and Mamie took me out to a café for a pastry afterward. They are very much in love. They told me they want to get married when they have enough money saved up. They will have the most beautiful children. Mamie has the most wonderful red hair and I told her she should never wear a wig. "Why would I do that? I'm a Yankee girl now!" she said.

October 8, 1904

Guess what? I am now an eighth grader. I have caught up with my age. I am so excited. Last week I did my recitation of Hiawatha and the teacher said I did very well, but still I am surprised. But she said that I can do eighth-grade math and can read and write so well that I should have no problem, and now Blu has been promoted, too. She is a sev-

enth grader but I think she will be in eighth grade by Purim. *I would love to tell Miriam I am an eighth grader now.*

October 15, 1904

I am so busy. I went with Mamie to see a hall where she and Boris might have their wedding in the springtime. Then she took me to a shop on Canal Street to look at beautiful fabric for her gown that she might buy. She said that since she has no mother or sisters she is making me her wedding advisor. Besides the wedding advising I still have much school work. Eighth grade is not easy. The easiest part is spelling. I have gotten 100 percent on every spelling test. Geography is hard. There is much to memorize — all the states and their capitals, lists of natural resources and agricultural products from every part the country. Then I must do a report on a President. We drew names out of a hat. I got Millard Fillmore. I never even heard of that President! And of course, I still am assistant prop girl. The show ends soon. I hope I get another job in another show.

October 18, 1904

Mama gets fatter everyday. This is going to be some big baby. She is happy, I can tell. She wants a boy, although she says just a healthy baby. I hope this baby doesn't take up too much time. What if I have to help take care of it the way Blu does with her mother? What if I have to give up my job at the theater? This job is the beginning of my career. I learned that new word this week. I like it. Career! It means more than a job. It means a life.

October 21, 1904

Big news! Wonderful news! Maybe the best news. Papa has been offered a full-time position teaching violin at the New York Conservatory of Music! He will make as much money as in the shop. But this is the other thing Papa did that is really making Mama happy. He did this before he even told us about the Conservatory. He will three nights a week help in Yitzy's father's shop. This really pleases Mama. It was very smart of Papa to do this. You see, I think that Mama does not really understand art. Mama thinks that to really earn money, to make a living, you must make something that you can hold in your hands and then sell. Like a cloak or a shirtwaist. Music slips through the air. *Music floats into your ears and then out again. The images that music makes, at least for Mama, vanish like clouds blown by the wind. So now Papa earns a living in two ways — one way for him and one way for Mama. They seem very happy.*

October 23, 1904

Minnie Leibowitz, the star of the show, got sick tonight after the second act. Her understudy had to go on. I could have done a better job. I know the lines better. I have been memorizing all the lines of all the actors — at least the girl actors, for just this reason. Of course, Minnie plays a completely grown-up woman. So it would be hard for them to put me in her part, but still someday somebody's going to get sick who is about my age and size and I shall be able to step into their shoes.

October 24, 1904

Who in the world is Millard Fillmore? I know he was President, but that is all. A lot of people don't even know he was President. I better find out something soon. The report is due in another week.

133

October 25, 1904

Boris to the rescue again. He took me uptown to the same place where Mandy took me for the information on Madame Curie, City College. We found a lot of things about Mr. Fillmore. He is still pretty boring. I wish I got Abraham Lincoln. Yetta Greenberg got Abraham Lincoln and believe me Lincoln is completely wasted on Yetta Greenberg. She is a dimwit. Isn't that the most wonderful American expression? It's so good it could almost be Yiddish.

October 30, 1904

Went uptown and spotted Miriam today. It is getting harder and harder for me to imagine speaking to her. I cannot figure this out. It is more than just that Mama would be angry with me.

November 1, 1904

I talked to Uncle Schmully about Miriam tonight. He told me something interesting. He says he is pretty sure that Papa has visited Miriam and has maybe even given her some money now that he is making more. He says Papa

won't say anything because he doesn't want to upset
Mama. So I say what a crazy family I live in. Nobody says
what they really are thinking or doing. We sneak around.
He says this is how families are. Half the time they argue
with one another and the other half of the time they tiptoe
around trying to protect each other for fear of hurting them.

It all seems very complicated to me.

November 2, 1904

I got a B on my Millard Fillmore report. The teacher
wrote on my paper, "Excellent spelling. Nice sentences,
well organized but too short." I felt like writing back,
"Millard Fillmore, in spite of living 74 years, had a very
boring life and could have done it in half the time." But
I did not write this.

November 7, 1904

Well, the Democratic precinct captain just paid us a visit.
He is so fat that the stairs creak as he climbs them and he
wheezes so much that we heard him long before he got here.
His trip is in vain of course, because Papa can't vote, but
he says if he could he would only vote for Mr. Roosevelt.
Papa and Tovah argue endlessly about this because Tovah

and all her union friends are Democrats. So round and round Papa and Tovah go. It's rather pointless as neither one can vote. But the way she goes on you'd think she could. Mama is horrified that a young lady would argue politics. But that of course wouldn't stop Tovah. "In Russia you wouldn't have done this," Mama says.

"In Russia there was no election to argue about," Tovah replies.

"It is unbecoming. How will we ever find you a husband with a mouth like that?" Mama wrings her hands, then pulls on her wig a bit.

Does this shut up my big sister? Never. "The only reason Papa would vote for Teddy Roosevelt is because Uncle Moishe made his Rough Rider suit for the Spanish-American War. Is this a democracy where a man, if he is rich enough, can have his uniform custom tailored at Brooks Brothers?" Tovah asks.

Then of course Papa chimes in, "That is not why I would vote for Mr. Roosevelt — I vote for the man, not the suit." He raises his finger as he says this and pauses because it does sound so good it maybe should be a headline. Then he continues. "But let me tell you, daughter, your Uncle Moishe made those canvas leggings look like cavalry twill and his skill in fashioning a cartridge pocket is to be matched by no one, I say no one on the Lower East Side. . . ."

I would definitely vote for Teddy Roosevelt if I could. But we will all go tomorrow with Uncle Moishe when he votes (Uncle Moishe is a citizen) and I don't care if it is boiling hot, I am going to wear the new winter coat that Mama fitted for me from one of the samples for Yitzy's father. It has velvet piping around the collar and both pockets. We Feldmans shall all walk proudly down Orchard Street to the polls, even though only Uncle Moishe can vote. Oh, how I wish the Tsar could see us now.

November 13, 1904

Guess what? I have a new play for which I shall be assistant prop girl. It is rumored that Jacob Adler is to be the star. I am so excited. Just imagine. I might be handing a prop to Jacob Adler!

P.S. Teddy Roosevelt won the election, but I am more excited about Jacob Adler.

November 14, 1904

Uncle Schmully confessed to me that he is in love with Blu's mother and they want to get married but first Mrs. Wolf must get a divorce. She will need a Jewish one from the rabbi and a United States one from the government. So I told Uncle Schmully about how Mama and I saw Mr. Wolf uptown. Uncle Schmully's eyes nearly popped out of his head when I told him this. Then I showed him the letter I wrote to the Jewish Daily Forward *and the answer. Uncle Schmully said that it was really important that I told him this. That now it might be quicker getting the divorce. Between Mamie taking me around to look at halls for her coming wedding and telling Uncle Schmully important things for his future marriage I guess I should go into the wedding advising business.*

November 17, 1904

Hanukkah *is just over two weeks away and I am not even excited. I wonder if* Miriam *will celebrate* Hanukkah?

I write for the first time in many weeks in Yiddish. No language except my own could hold these feelings. And yet I am numb. My fingers move mechanically with the pen across this page as I tell this terrible story. It is the worst tragedy I have ever known. Mamie is dead. She died in a terrible fire at the Diamond Shirtwaist Factory where she worked. Yesterday when school let out Blu and I walked up Ludlow toward Hester Street and it seemed unusually quiet and empty. For the first few minutes we were just perplexed and then we saw tight little knots of people standing together on street corners talking in low voices. But suddenly Blu and I both noticed that there were hardly any carts or wagons. Usually there is a tangle of carts and wagons clogging the streets near and around Hester Street. "What's happening?" Blu asked someone. A terrible fire, near Washington Square, they said. The Diamond Shirtwaist Factory. I screamed for I knew that was where Mamie worked. I grabbed Blu's hand and we tore through the streets. It had been very cold and there was ice and sometimes we slipped.

Soon we saw huge black clouds of smoke and ashes and cinders swirling through the air. The factory was in a big loft building that took up an entire block. I gasped as I saw flames leaping out of the windows and from the roof. We pushed our way into the crowd and looked up. Mamie! I whispered her name. Blu and I held on to each other and looked up in horror. "The doors are locked," someone said. "What?" I turned and asked. "Why?" "They don't like workers leaving early," another person said. "So now they jump from the windows." And sure enough just at that moment I saw a figure hurl through the air and then I saw a couple standing in a window fringed with flames. I watched them wrap themselves in each other's arms and fall. "We got nets!" a cry came out. I felt the crowd surge backward. "They need room, the firemen need room to spread the nets!" a voice boomed through a megaphone. The bodies continued to fall from the windows. Workers leaped and dived and jumped out of the flames but most were killed hitting the ground. The fire burned for more than an hour before the firemen could break into the building.

Blu and I stayed for hours. I kept praying that Mamie would get out and that we would see her. But with each minute my hopes dwindled. Finally we each went home and I could only hope that maybe she had gotten out and we had missed her. I told Mama what had happened. She put her hand over her mouth, and her eyes grew wide. "Tovah!" she whispered. "No, Mama. It was not Tovah's factory. Not anywhere near it."

None of us could go to sleep. Papa came back early from the Conservatory for he had heard, and Uncle Schmully came back early from work, too. We all sat around. We ate no dinner. Finally, close to midnight, Tovah came in. It was as if her face had caved in. Very quietly she said, "One hundred workers dead." "Mamie?" I asked. "Is Mamie dead?" I could barely get out the word. Tovah's head seemed to sink into her shoulders. There was this terrible shudder that went like a current through her whole body. And I knew that Mamie, my dear beautiful Mamie with the hair like a sunset, was dead.

I don't want to write anymore. It might be a long time before I write again.

January 16, 1905

Nearly two months since I have written, since the terrible fire. Mamie is gone nearly two months. It is still unbelievable to me. I try not to think about it, but it is hard. I see Boris all the time at the theater, but he is like a shadow of a man, a ghost. His eyes are dim and hollow. Tovah now works day and night with her union to try and make laws that will prevent a terrible thing like this from ever happening again. But still Mamie is gone. I know what dead is now. Dead is not Miriam up on 110th Street married to a Catholic man. Dead is Mamie. Smashed on the pavement. Her blood soaking into the ice, the snowy gutters. That is dead.

I still work in the theater three nights a week. It is a rest to enter this magical world but even this takes effort now.

January 20, 1905

There has begun in Russia a little over a week ago a big revolution. It started on a Sunday in front of the Winter Palace in St. Petersburg when the Tsar ordered demonstrators in a peaceful march to be gunned down. They now call this day Bloody Sunday. Uncle Schmully took me to his club. It is called the Lermontov Club and there are a lot of his old friends from the Bund in it. They jabber about revolution. They are all very excited. I myself thought it was boring. I know revolution is very exciting but sitting around talking about it isn't. They all smoke too much. I could hardly breathe.

January 22, 1905

I have felt so empty since Mamie died. I walk around. I see, I think. I do my schoolwork. I talk with Blu and Yitzy. But nothing really touches me, makes me excited or happy. I mean, you know I work in the theater and my dream of handing Jacob Adler a prop. Well, that dream has come true. A year ago I would die to do this. It means so little to me now. Will I ever be normal again? I would talk to Uncle Schmully about it but I don't know what to say. And what could he do? He is so in love. Why should I spoil his happiness with my problems? I feel so alone. So terribly alone.

February 1, 1905

Something pretty good has happened. Yes, a dream come true. I am going to have a part in a play. I am excited. I really am. But I still am not feeling the way I would have a year ago and that saddens me. But I think I must act — really act now, if I am to do a good job. I must pretend that this is the most wonderful thing that ever happened even though now I would trade the part in a minute if Mamie could come back. The play is Shulamith, *the very first Yiddish play that I ever saw, and I get to be one of Shulamith's children. The one who gets eaten by a lion. That is the best one to play because if I was the other one, the child who gets thrown down the well, I just disappear in a flash, but I have more time on stage. The lion wrestles me to the ground and then clamps me in his jaws and drags me off the stage. There is plenty of acting time. So I am going to work very hard and practice expressions of horror and pain that one might have if being eaten alive by a lion.*

February 10, 1905

It is not easy being eaten by a lion. I have bruises all over me. Two men play the lion, one is the front and one is the back. They are under a furry cover with a head, a huge head with papier-mâché teeth as long as bananas. My head fits inside the lion's head. The costume designer made it that way on purpose because it is so dramatic to see my head being eaten that way. But I face the audience so they can see my looks of horror. I practice my horror looks every night in the mirror. The play opens two weeks before Purim. So we have almost a month to rehearse.

February 15, 1905

Blu came and watched me in rehearsal after school and she said Jacob Adler was backstage and he was watching me,

144

too, and he said to the stage manager, "That little girl is good. Look even here in this scene when she is quiet you see her concern for her mother — that's good acting." Oh, my goodness, I cannot believe he really said that. I have to think hard about what I was doing in that scene.

February 19, 1905

Guess what? Mama had her baby. A boy! We are all so happy. He came a little early, but he is a dear little fellow. Rather red and wrinkly and very tiny. We are calling him Yossel. In English Yossel is Joseph. But Mama says we shall not call him Joey. I am much more excited than I thought I would be. Blu's mother came with a midwife to help deliver the baby. It was a quick delivery. Mama did so well. She is just beaming all the time now. She keeps saying, "A little boy!" She talks to him and says, "You will be a gaon, *a gifted scholar of the Talmud." I don't spoil her thoughts, but I don't think boys growing up around Orchard Street want to be* gaons *anymore. There are too many other things to want to be in America. Mandy told me that he had wanted to be a Talmudic scholar before he came to America. In fact he had never read any other books but the Talmud but then he began reading. First he was, in his own words, "gulping" down Charles Dickens and many*

English writers. Then he discovered higher mathematics and chemistry. These held mysteries and puzzles that were as intriguing as those of the Talmud. So now Mandy goes in the evening to City College and studies chemistry and one day might be a doctor. I wouldn't mind having a little brother who is a doctor.

Tonight I come home from rehearsal and I simply cannot believe this — our little Yossel is gone. He died three hours ago. It being Sunday I was at rehearsal all day. When I left Mama thought he felt a little feverish. By afternoon it had gotten worse. Papa ran for a doctor. But by the time the doctor got here it was too late and little Yossel had turned blue. The doctor said that because he came early his lungs were probably not strong enough. So when he caught a cold it was just as if the little lungs filled up with water and he drowned. Mama sits very still. She cries but no sound comes out. Papa just holds her hand. I wish they had not told me what the doctor said about little Yossel drowning. I hate that picture. After Mamie died I kept picturing her face smashed on the icy pavement. Death can be over in a matter of seconds for the victim but for the living it is like one long forever streaming with images.

February 27, 1905

I wonder if Miriam knows about Mama. I wonder if she ever even knew Mama was expecting. I must begin to think about doing something with Miriam. This cannot go on forever. But what should I do?

March 4, 1905

It is really awful in our house. Mama is in another world. She does not sew. She hardly eats. Now I am worried that Uncle Schmully might want to leave. I mean it is such a sad place where we live. If Uncle Schmully goes I shall just be lost. Papa is so busy with Mama and Tovah with the union. Uncle Schmully is the only one who knows I am alive. He says he will come to my opening performance — less than a week away. I know Mama is not well enough and Papa will stay with Mama and Tovah cannot come because she has a meeting, but she promises to come the second night. As much as I love Uncle Schmully I would like some of my very own family there.

March 5, 1905

Three days to go before my opening. I am concentrating so hard on everything I must remember onstage. I know all my lines perfectly. I do not have that many but I keep thinking what if my mind goes blank and I open my mouth and nothing comes out?

March 6, 1905

Two days to go before my opening. I wonder if Boris will come by. He is working in another theater.

March 7, 1905

One day before my opening. I am so nervous. This the first real step in my career. What if it ends suddenly? Things happen. One can never tell. Look at little Yossel. Look at Mamie. Her life over before she could even get the hall for her wedding. I should not talk this way because I am not worried about dying, just making a mistake and ending my career before it begins. That is not so bad as dying, I guess. Oh, I want so much to do well. I want to pray to God, please God — no more surprises. Just let me do well.

March 9, 1905
After midnight

I must again write in Yiddish for my heart is too full —
full not with pain but finally joy. Oh, yes, the performance went well. I did not forget any of my lines,
but at the end of the first act, when I was more relaxed
and could look out from the wings into the audience,
who should I see sitting in the fifth row to the right
but Miriam and Sean! They came to see me! Uncle
Schmully was two rows ahead so I do not even know if
he saw them at first. I started to weep. Leni Fein, who
plays Shulamith, comes up to me and says (she talks
English in this funny Yiddish accent, New York style)
"Vhat's you cryin' about? You ain't been et yet by the
lion." I try to explain, but just blubber. Then Boris sees
me. He comes over. I take one look and understand that
he knows everything; that he is the one who brought
them here. And he says simply, "That they should miss
this night of yours — never! They should see the first
glow of what might be a star in the heavens of Yiddish
theater."

"I'm no star, Boris." I blubber some more.

"It all begins with a twinkle," he says and pinches
my cheek. "Now go out there and act."

And that is exactly what I do. I remember what Jacob Adler said about how even when I was still he could sense the pain I felt for my mother, and I indeed thought of my poor mother grieving for her little Yossel, her hope for a *gaon*. And then when the lion takes me in his mouth I think of the blood in the snowy gutters and the ice melting red. And at the end of the play I take my bow. And Miriam and Sean are standing up and yelling and clapping and cheering.

I cannot remember what happened next exactly except Miriam and I were backstage hugging and Sean was hugging Uncle Schmully and then suddenly Uncle Schmully says, "Miriam, Sean, you must come back to Orchard Street with us. We must stop all this nonsense. Life is too short." So through the sleeting night we all go back. And we know Uncle Schmully is right. We just know it. So we almost run. We are running up the stairs of number 14 Orchard. We are running down the hall.

"Mama!" Miriam shouts as she bursts through the door with Sean right behind her. "Mama, I am alive. You cannot make me dead. Mama, I am alive and I love you." And Mama touches her hand to her head to adjust her wig but then she remembers she is only wearing a scarf. And her hand just stays in midair. And she makes the shape of Miriam's name on her lips. And then she whispers "Mirmela," for that is her baby name for Miriam as mine is Zippola and Tovah's is Tovəla. And she says it again and suddenly it is as if Mama has flown across the room. And she wraps her arms around Miriam and she hugs her so tight. And then she breaks away and she looks at Sean and she says a Tanta Fruma: "Love and hunger do not live together. My Miriam looks healthy and beautiful." She takes Sean's hand and presses it to her lips.

Then everyone cries and cries and cries. One minute later Tovah comes in. And for the first time in her entire existence Tovah is absolutely speechless. It is actually Tanta Fruma who has the last word — through my mother's mouth. Mama says, "You get as old as a cow but you still go on learning."

So I am calmer now and can write once more in English. I only have one page left in this diary that Mama bought for me back in Zarichka. As I write, it feels as if I am at the end of what has been a very long night or maybe it is the beginning of a new day. I look back in this diary I have kept now for over a year — eighteen months to be exact, and I think this is a very strange sort of story. It begins with an ending, the ending of our life in Russia, and it ends with a beginning. And throughout the entire diary there are beginnings and endings that seem to braid together like a plait of very long hair. Sometimes one cannot tell the beginning from the ending and this is not necessarily bad for if one really knew one might not have the courage to go on. I want to go on. I think I shall buy a new diary tomorrow and begin to fill it up with my story. I am sure there will be many more beginnings and endings and I hope that I shall never be quite sure which is which.

Epilogue

Zipporah ended her formal education after two years of high school. By that time she was getting steady work on the stage. In the same year her father was able to stop working in the needle trade entirely as he was invited to join the New York Philharmonic Orchestra as first violinist. The Feldmans moved uptown a few years later to live closer to Carnegie Hall. Sarah Feldman continued to work in custom dressmaking for uptown ladies for several years. She never gave up her Jewish wig. Tovah's union became part of the International Ladies Garment Workers Union, and Tovah worked her way up through the ranks and became secretary of the organization. She was well known as a strike organizer and was a frequent contributor to the *Jewish Daily Forward*, writing about socialist causes. Miriam and Sean had four children and eventually moved to Brooklyn, where Sean became a fire chief.

Indeed, Zippy's role in *Shulamith* as the child eaten by the lion was just the very beginning of a long and illustrious career in the Yiddish theater. Zipporah

Feldman became one of the New York Yiddish theater's most beloved stars. Her mother worried that neither one of her daughters would ever settle down and marry. Tovah never did. But finally after what Sarah Feldman called the world's longest courtship, Zippy and Yitzy Silver married in 1920. She was almost thirty years old. Yitzy had by this time become a millionaire as one of the largest women's cloak manufacturers in the country. Zipporah and Yitzy had three children, all boys. One, Yossel, joined his mother in the theater. One became a doctor, and the third joined his father in the cloak business.

Zipporah's most distinguished role on the stage was that of the widow in the Jewish *Queen Lear*. She was hailed by critics throughout the world on her European tour in 1930. By 1939 World War II had broken out. Zippy and Yitzy worked feverishly to help Jewish children get out of Germany and escape the Nazis. They contributed hundreds of thousands of dollars to various Jewish relief organizations and after the war Zipporah was honored by the Hadassah, an organization of Jewish women in America.

In 1940 at the age of fifty and at the pinnacle of her acting career, Zipporah made her first Hollywood movie. *A Treacherous Woman* told the story of an undercover Russian revolutionary who works as the governess to the Tsar's children and helps plot the downfall of the Russian monarchy. For her role Zippy was nominated for an Academy Award. She lost to Ginger Rogers, who won for the movie *Kitty Foyle*. She was disappointed she didn't win but as she told her grandchildren in later years, "Not winning an Oscar wasn't the end. It was just a beginning." She was subsequently in ten more motion pictures and she and Yitzy bought a home in Beverly Hills, California, with a swimming pool and tennis courts. She learned how to swim at the age of fifty-two and took up tennis that year as well.

Zipporah Feldman lived a very long life, which was rich with beginnings and endings and much in between. When she was well into her eighties she attended the stage debut of her great-granddaughter Fruma in the role of Mary Magdalen in Andrew Lloyd Webber's musical *Jesus Christ Superstar*. She was interviewed at the theater by Barbara Walters who asked her, "What does the first lady of Yiddish theater think of her great-granddaughter debuting in a play like *Jesus Christ Superstar*?" "I loved it!" replied Zippy. "Who wouldn't want to see her granddaughter singing and dancing so beautifully on the Broadway stage? Are you crazy? It's a wonderful role. Mary Magdalen was a very misunderstood Jewish girl. We would all do well to try to understand her story. That is what theater is about. Understanding human stories."

Life in America
in 1903

Historical Note

Jews lived a precarious existence in nineteenth-century Russia. They were required, by law, to stay in a designated area called the Pale of Settlement. Not permitted in the major industrial cities and limited to particular trades, most Jews found it difficult to make a living. Jewish men were arbitrarily drafted into the army, separating them from their families for years. In general, Jews were looked on with suspicion or outright hatred. When Tsar Alexander II was assassinated in 1881, the murder was blamed on all Jews. The soldiers of the Tsar, called *Cossacks,* began a wave of *pogroms*, attacks against Jews. Without warning, Cossacks would suddenly gallop on horseback into a sleeping village, rape and murder the inhabitants, and then burn down their homes. *Pogroms* were horrifying, destructive expressions of anti-Semitism.

In whispers, the word began to circulate that America was a place where Jews were welcome. It was called "The Golden Country," because the streets were said to be paved with gold. Reluctant to leave their homeland, but fearing for their lives, over two million Russian Jews migrated to the United States between the late 1880s and 1924.

Although Jews lived throughout the country, in the West, the South and the Midwest, the largest number of Jews settled in sections of New York City, particularly on the Lower East Side of Manhattan. In the late 1800s and early 1900s, approximately 350,000 Jews lived within two square miles. They lived in dark, cramped tenements in unsanitary conditions where disease was a constant threat. It was uncomfortable and unpleasant, but at least Jews were physically safe from Cossacks and *pogroms*.

It may have been disappointing to realize that American streets were not paved with gold, but a person who worked hard could earn a better living in America than was possible in Russia. Many young men borrowed money to buy pushcarts, worked as peddlers on the street, and in time were able to save enough of their earnings to open their own stores. With no real option to return home, Russian Jews put all their energies toward succeeding in their adopted country.

For those who had difficulty, there were *landsmanshafts*. In the Jewish tradition of charity, these organizations, created by people from the same *shtetl*, or hometown, provided for the sick, for a little financial help when needed, and for funerals. Sometimes a synagogue was part of a *landsmanshaft*. But unfortunately, these organizations didn't last very long, partly because immigrants didn't want to be associated with the old ways or with the Old Country. They wanted to be American. There was pride in being an American.

America was seen as a great "melting pot," an ideal place where all individuals were an important part of the mix, no matter what their national or ethnic origins. Each person may have been considered equal by law, but in fact, people tended to stay with their own, and in the crowded neighborhoods there were often conflicts among the Irish, the Italians, the Polish, and various other groups. Still, immigrants were encouraged to adopt the American lifestyle, and everyone believed that material prosperity and social position were possible if you worked hard enough.

But, while some people were prospering, many were struggling and even starving. When photojournalists like Lewis Hine and Jacob Riis documented the squalid conditions of poor immigrants, there was a public outcry demanding that something be done to improve living standards. Politicians advocated social reforms. Wealthy Americans, perhaps with a thinly disguised sense of superiority, volunteered their services and held fabulous charity balls. A variety of social, educational, health care, and welfare agencies were founded to help the less fortunate. To the Russian Jews, who valued and respected education, one of the most important, and particularly American, institutions was the public library. The new immigrants gratefully borrowed books and used the quiet rooms as a place to study and sit with friends. They were impressed with the American notion that everyone should be educated and eagerly took advantage of the public programs available to them. Adults went to night school to learn English and sent their children to public school. In their zeal for their children to assimilate and become American, parents stopped teaching them Yiddish and, unfortunately, the colorfully expressive language is hardly spoken by anyone today.

German Jews, many of whom had immigrated to America in the 1820s, hired the newer Russian Jewish immigrants to work as tailors, seamstresses, general workers, and salesmen in their ready-made clothes businesses, called the "needle trades." Some Jewish workers who had brought socialist ideas with them from Russia began to complain about their cruel exploitation in sweatshops. As early as the 1880s, these self-appointed labor leaders raised questions of workers' rights. A Jewish organization, The Workmen's Circle, was one of the first to set up a system of workers' insurance and benefits, and it also served as a center of social activity. They tried to organize all workers, not just Jews, and rallied for the formation of trade unions. To most workers, these ideas seemed too revolutionary, and they weren't willing to risk their paychecks by being associated with a union. When 60,000 cloakmakers of the International Ladies Garment Workers Union went on strike, Louis D. Brandeis was called in to mediate between workers and employers. It was a milestone in the history of U.S. labor. Trade unions proved that they were a force. They had status. But then in 1911 the tragic Triangle Shirtwaist factory fire killed 146 workers, mostly women and girls, who had been locked inside the factory unable to escape the terrible blaze. This single incident created such great public sympathy for the workers' cause that many felt encouraged to demonstrate and hold strikes.

For the Jewish community, this was a lively period of social and philosophical interaction. There were sports events, concerts, scholarly lectures, socials and dances, Yiddish newspapers, thriving Yiddish theaters, and exhilarating outlets for artists and intellectuals. The excitement of the times caused a tremendous conflict for individual Jews, as it has for many American immigrants. Young people were torn between the traditional religious and social practices of their ancestors and the liberal choices of a new, vibrant American society. Jewish family pressures exerted an extremely strong influence but, finally, many traditions gave way.

During the years 1880 to 1929, people from all over the world moved to America in unprecedented numbers. In the 1920s, there was a backlash against the continuing influx of "foreigners," and the first act to restrict immigration was passed in 1921. Following that, the Immigration Act of 1924 created stricter requirements and quotas for all those wishing to move to the United States. Immigration from every country was severely curtailed, and Asian workers were denied entry completely. The period of spectacular immigration population growth and expansion had come to an end. But, by then, Russian Jews had been absorbed into American society. Many succeeded in a number of fields and influenced law, medicine, finance, music, literature, and theater. One Russian-Jewish immigrant who made a great impact was Louis B. Mayer, co-founder of Metro Goldwyn Mayer and a developer of one of the most essentially American products, the Hollywood movie.

Despite the struggles, hard work, and anti-Semitic prejudice, many Russian-Jewish immigrants found a level of success in America. America may not have been what they originally expected, but it might be said that it turned out to be a kind of Golden Country after all.

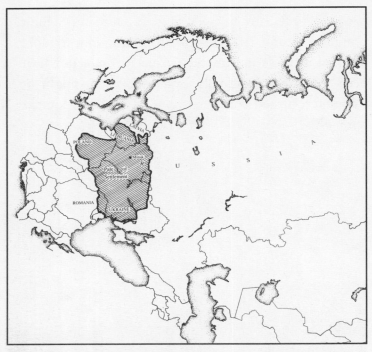

Russia proper was over 6 million square miles in area, so although the Pale of Settlement—the only place Jews were permitted to live during this time in history—may appear to be a large territory, it was only a portion (386,100 square miles) of the country. Numerous anti-Semitic decrees that curtailed Jewish activities and professions made life within the Pale difficult and often unpleasant for Jews. The Pale was abolished in 1917 when the Russian Revolution ended.

As many as two million Jews immigrated to the United States between 1880 and 1924. Many were so poor that they could only afford to travel in steerage where conditions were uncomfortably crowded and terribly unsanitary.

After an arduous journey, the new immigrants faced one more anxious trial before being permitted to enter America: the medical exam. Trachoma was a common, very contagious eye disease. Immigrants with any contagious disease were immediately returned to their country of origin.

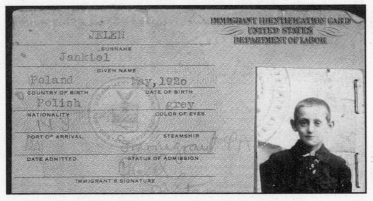

Each new immigrant was given an American identity card. In many cases, American names were given to immigrants by overworked clerks at Ellis Island who, not familiar with the foreign names, wrote down what they thought they heard. Today, it is possible to meet cousins whose family names are spelled differently or even changed considerably.

Poor immigrants lived in dark, crowded tenement buildings. Often more than one family shared an apartment, sometimes adding a boarder or two to help pay the rent. There was only one bathroom shared by all the apartments on a floor, tubs in the kitchen, and, too frequently, vermin in the hallways.

On the Lower East Side, as depicted here in George Benjamin Luks's painting of Hester Street, people naturally preferred the streets to their cramped living quarters.

Peddlers sold their wares from pushcarts; young people socialized; and men and women bargained and gossiped while their children ran around under the watchful eyes of the whole neighborhood.

Even poor girls paid attention to fashion, and most tried to look as American as possible. A new immigrant (called a "greenhorn") was easily spotted and often teased. For young girls, like these pictured, the fashion of the times included large hair bows.

Impromptu street games were commonly played by neighborhood kids, especially in the summer months when it stayed light into the evening. Without much money for entertainment, they used their imaginations to find ways to have fun.

Poor immigrant families were especially delighted with the American ideal of public education for everyone. Parents pressed their children to do well in school and most importantly to learn to be good Americans and absorb American values.

Many Russian Jews worked in the garment business in sweat shops, which were probably named for the fact that they were hot, airless places where people sweated while they sewed and stitched. When a few of these Jewish workers convinced their coworkers to band together and ask for better working conditions, labor unions were created.

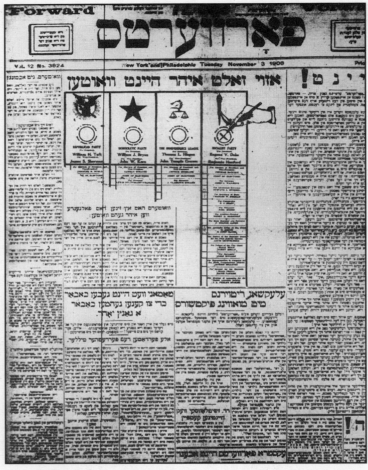

The Jewish Daily Forward *was the most popular Yiddish newspaper. Its provocative editorials caused daily discussions on street corners and in cafés. The* Forward *is still published today, in English, Russian, and Yiddish. Originally an oral language, Yiddish borrowed the Hebrew alphabet when it was written down, as shown here in the newspaper's Yiddish edition.*

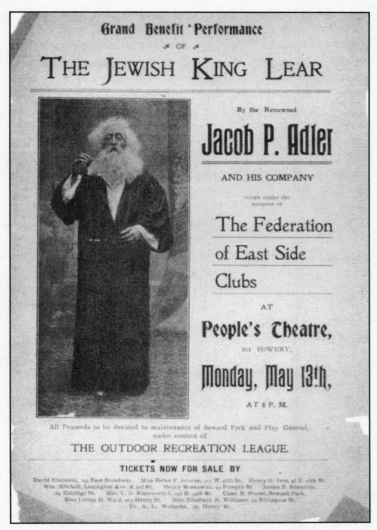

Jews frequently went to the Yiddish theater to see melodramas about the immigrant experience, as well as Yiddish versions of the classics.

The synagogue was the center of the social and religious community for Jews of the Lower East Side. The Eldridge Street Synagogue pictured here is one of the oldest on the Lower East Side and is a historical landmark.

HAMANTASCHEN

Ingredients:

4 cups all-purpose flour
½ teaspoon salt
1 cup sugar
2 teaspoons baking powder
3 eggs

1 teaspoon vanilla
⅓ cup butter
⅓ cup orange juice
flour for rolling dough
prune or apricot filling

Directions:

1. Preheat oven to 350 degrees.
2. Sift flour, salt, and baking powder.
3. Cream butter and sugar.
4. Slowly add vanilla, eggs, and orange juice to butter and sugar mixture. Add dry ingredients.
5. Knead dough until smooth.
6. Roll out dough with rolling pin on floured surface until ¼" thick.
7. Use cookie cutter to make circles of dough.
8. Follow diagram below.
9. Bake for twenty minutes or until lightly brown.
   Makes about 3 dozen Hamantaschen.

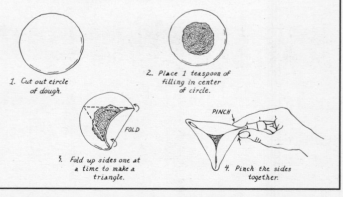

1. Cut out circle of dough.

2. Place 1 teaspoon of filling in center of circle.

3. Fold up sides one at a time to make a triangle.

PINCH

4. Pinch the sides together.

Religion was essential and deeply important to the Russian Jewish immigrants. Their lives revolved around the celebration of the weekly Sabbath and numerous holidays. A favorite holiday was Purim. Triangular-shaped cookies called Hamantaschen were baked with a variety of tasty fillings.

SHALOM ALEICHEM

"Shalom Aleichem" is traditionally sung at the dinner table to welcome the Sabbath, the Jewish day of rest.

1. This is my hope and my prayer
   Let there be peace everywhere,
   Let there be joy for all to share,
   And let us praise the Lord and
   live a happy life!

2. I'm saying "Shalom Aleichem!"
   I'm praying "Shalom Aleichem!"
   Proclaiming "Shalom Aleichem!"
   So let us praise the Lord and
   live a happy life!

3. I'm singing "Shalom Aleichem!"
   Bells ringing "Shalom Aleichem!"
   Keep singing "Shalom Aleichem!"
   So let us praise the Lord and
   live a happy life!

4. Hear this plea . . . you'll agree . . .
   You will see . . . harmony . . .
   Merrily, joyfully, happily, playfully,
   Sing along with me!

5. Come on and sing, Hallelujah!
   For it will bring glory to ya,
   A ting-g'l-ing will tingle thru ya,
   So let us praise the Lord and
   live a happy life!

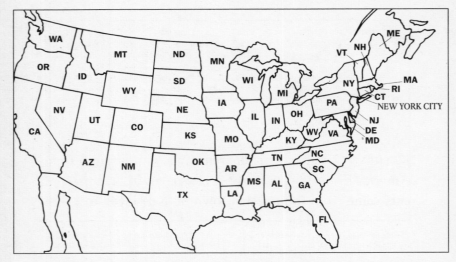

Modern map of the United States showing the approximate location of New York City.

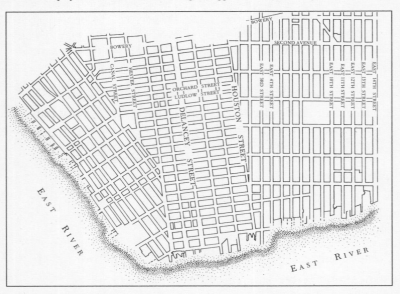

This detail of Manhattan shows the main streets of the Lower East Side that are mentioned in the diary. Over 350,000 Jewish immigrants lived within two square miles of land during this time in American history.

About the Author

KATHRYN LASKY's grandparents all immigrated to America from Eastern Europe. Her paternal grandparents came from the Russian town of Nikolayev to escape the pogroms and conscription into the Tsar's armies. Unlike Zippy and her family, they did not come through Ellis Island and live on the Lower East Side. Instead, they came through Canada and settled in Minnesota. "But no matter where immigrants came from or where they lived," Lasky says, "there were common experiences and immense challenges.

"My grandparents had all died by the time I was three, but that did not prevent me from asking my parents about their journeys to America. And I still had aunts and uncles who remembered. To me the most amazing thing of all was that they had arrived in this country and could not speak a word of English. How had the children learned this new language? How had they made friends? Fit into school? My aunts and uncles told me that within months the children were speaking better English than the parents. As a child, this intrigued me. There were very few things I could do better than my parents.

"By the time my sister and I were born, my parents no longer spoke Yiddish very well, though it was still spoken often in my grandparents' homes. To be able to read American literature, and write and speak English was as important as making a lot of money. My own mother who was not a boastful type, once said when a grandchild of hers got a B+ on an English composition, 'No member of our family has ever received below an A- in English since we got off the boat!'

"I loved writing the diary of Zipporah Feldman. For me, the most fun was doing the research. In one immigrant reminiscence I read about the trick of turning a jacket inside out if the health inspectors had marked it with one of the dreaded letters that indicated illness. I read the horrendous account of the Triangle Shirtwaist factory fire, which occurred in the year 1911. I used it as the basis for the fictional Diamond Factory fire in which Mamie died. I pored over hundreds of wonderful pictures taken by Jacob Riis and other photographers and studied the fascinating faces of these brave children and the appalling conditions of their tenement apartments. I looked for the light of hope in their eyes, the trace of mischief in a fleeting smile. Sometimes I found it, sometimes I didn't.

"But the very best part of writing this diary was that it was a way of connecting with my aunts, uncles, and grandparents whom I had only known as elderly gray-haired ladies and men. And yet even then I'd been able to detect the sparkle within their faded eyes. It was the sparkle of immigrants and true adventurers."

Kathyrn Lasky is the author of more than forty books for children and adults, including one other book in the Dear America series, *A Journey to the New World: The Diary of Remember Patience Whipple*, an NCSS Notable Children's Trade Book in the Field of Social Studies and an *American Bookseller* Pick of the Lists. She has written about the immigrant experiences of her own family in her book *The Night Journey*, winner of the National Jewish Book Award, and in *Marven of the Great North Woods*. She won a Newbery Honor for her book *Sugaring Time*.

For Nat and Lochi Glazer

Acknowledgments

Grateful acknowledgment is made for permission to reprint the following:

Cover portrait: "Amarilla" by Frederick Lord Leighton (1830–1896). Collection of Christie's Images, A Division of Christie's Inc., Long Island City, New York.

Cover background: "Hester Street" by George Benjamin Luks (1867–1933). Oil on canvas, 66.3" x 91.8". Collection of Brooklyn Museum of Art, Brooklyn, New York.

Page 166: Map of the Pale of Settlement by Heather Saunders.

Page 167: Immigrants on ship, Library of Congress.

Page 168 (top): Eye examination, National Park Service, Statue of Liberty National Monument, Liberty Island, New York, New York.

Page 168 (bottom): Immigrant identification card, ibid.

Page 169 (top): Tenement flat, photograph by Jacob Riis, Corbis-Bettman, New York, New York.

Page 169 (bottom): "Hester Street" by George Benjamin Luks, Brooklyn Museum of Art, Brooklyn, New York.

Page 170: Hester Street, Museum of the City of New York, New York, New York.

Page 172: Children playing ball, George Eastman House, Rochester, New York.

Other Books in the *Dear America* Series

A Journey to the New World
The Diary of Remember Patience Whipple
by Kathryn Lasky

The Winter of Red Snow
The Revolutionary War Diary of Abigail Jane Stewart
by Kristiana Gregory

When Will This Cruel War Be Over?
The Civil War Diary of Emma Simpson
by Barry Denenberg

A Picture of Freedom
The Diary of Clotee, a Slave Girl
by Patricia C. McKissack

Across the Wide and Lonesome Prairie
The Oregon Trail Diary of Hattie Campbell
by Kristiana Gregory

So Far from Home
The Diary of Mary Driscoll, an Irish Mill Girl
by Barry Denenberg

I Thought My Soul Would Rise and Fly
The Diary of Patsy, a Freed Girl
by Joyce Hansen

West to a Land of Plenty
The Diary of Teresa Angelino Viscardi
by Jim Murphy

While the events described and some of the characters in this book
may be based on actual historical events and real people, Zipporah
Feldman is a fictional character, created by the author; her diary and
its epilogue are works of fiction.

Copyright © 1998 by Kathryn Lasky.

All rights reserved. Published by Scholastic Inc.
557 Broadway, New York, New York 10012.
DEAR AMERICA®, SCHOLASTIC, and associated logos
are trademarks and/or registered trademarks of Scholastic Inc.

Library of Congress Cataloging-in-Publication Data available.

ISBN 0-590-02973-8;
ISBN 0-439-44563-9 (pbk.)

10 9 8 7 6 5 4 3 2   02 03 04 05 06

The display type was set in Bodoni.
The text type was set in Fournier.
Book design by Elizabeth B. Parisi

Printed in the U.S.A. 23
First paperback printing, October 2002